**"Thanks again, Rory.
For everything," Goldie said.**

He stared at her for a moment, then waved goodbye and left.

Goldie closed her eyes and remembered the hominess of Rory's rambling farmhouse, the cute grins of his two boys—wait, the cute grin of the youngest boy, since the older one had seemed a bit sad—and the way Rory's eyes crinkled when he smiled. And she imagined the kind of woman who could be part of that lovely picture. The kind of woman who baked cookies and kept the house neat and played kick ball with the boys in the backyard. That kind of loving, caring, motherly type of woman.

And then she reminded herself that she'd come to Viola, Louisiana, to help her grandmother, not get involved with yet another man who probably didn't know the meaning of the words trust and commitment.

No matter how kind Rory Branagan had been, and no matter how much her heart was telling her that this man might just be different from all the rest.

Books by Lenora Worth

Love Inspired

The Wedding Quilt
Logan's Child
I'll Be Home for Christmas
Wedding at Wildwood
His Brother's Wife
Ben's Bundle of Joy
The Reluctant Hero
One Golden Christmas
†*When Love Came to Town*
†*Something Beautiful*
†*Lacey's Retreat*
Easter Blessings
"The Lily Field"
‡*The Carpenter's Wife*
‡*Heart of Stone*
‡*A Tender Touch*
Blessed Bouquets
"The Dream Man"
**A Certain Hope*
**A Perfect Love*
**A Leap of Faith*
Christmas Homecoming
Mountain Sanctuary
Lone Star Secret
Gift of Wonder
The Perfect Gift

†In the Garden
‡Sunset Island
*Texas Hearts

Love Inspired Suspense

Fatal Image
Secret Agent Minister
Deadly Texas Rose
A Face in the Shadows
Heart of the Night
Code of Honor

Steeple Hill

After the Storm
Echoes of Danger
Once Upon a Christmas
"Twas the Week Before Christmas"

LENORA WORTH

has written more than thirty books, most of those for Steeple Hill. She also works freelance for a local magazine, where she had written monthly opinion columns, feature articles and social commentaries. She also wrote for the local paper for five years. Married to her high school sweetheart for thirty-three years, Lenora lives in Louisiana and has two grown children and a cat. She loves to read, take long walks and sit in her garden.

The Perfect Gift

Lenora Worth

Published by Steeple Hill Books™

STEEPLE HILL BOOKS

ISBN-13: 978-0-373-87555-9

THE PERFECT GIFT

This edition published by arrangement with Steeple Hill Books.

www.SteepleHill.com

Printed in U.S.A.

Every good and perfect gift is from above, coming down from the Father of the heavenly lights, who does not change like shifting shadows.

—*James* 1:17

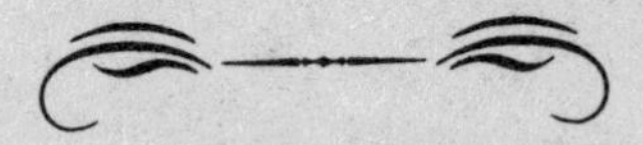

To the Unity Sunday School class—
for all their good and perfect gifts.

Prologue

The man and the two little boys stared down at the disheveled woman asleep on the big Ultrasuede couch in their living room.

"Is she a princess, Daddy?" six-year-old Tyler asked, his dark eyes going wide. "My friend Emily is always talking about princesses. She's a girl, though." He shrugged. "I don't know much about that kind of stuff."

"She's not a princess, silly," his older brother, Sam, answered with ten-year-old authority. "And she shouldn't be here. Isn't it illegal to enter someone's house when they're not at home, Dad? Besides, she's ruining our couch with her wet clothes."

Rory, still in shock from finding the woman there in the first place, stopped staring and went into action. "It's okay, Sam. She looks hurt." He gently nudged at the woman's arm. "Ma'am, excuse me? Wake up, okay?" When the woman didn't move, he panicked. "Lady, can you hear me?"

"She's asleep," Tyler pointed out. "Maybe she needs a blanket."

Rory pushed away the blanket his son offered. "Let's make sure she's all right first." He bent and carefully rolled the woman over from her stomach to her back, then felt for a pulse along her neck. She had a pulse. That much he knew. He could feel it through the softness of her skin. And she was wearing an intricate gold-chained square locket that fell across her V-necked sweater with each movement of her breath.

"Is she dead?" Sam asked, his curiosity with all things crime-related making Rory wince. The kid had been that way since his mother had been killed three years earlier in a convenience-store robbery.

"No, son. She's breathing. But something is definitely wrong."

Rory carefully examined the woman for broken bones or any other signs of injury, then turned her face around so he could inspect it. And that's when he saw the blood matted in her dark blond hair just above her left temple.

"She don't look so great," Tyler remarked.

"No, she doesn't," Rory replied, grabbing his cell out of his pocket. He immediately called 911 and explained the situation. "We found a woman in our house, unconscious and bleeding from a head wound. She needs medical attention."

After giving his address to the dispatcher, Rory hung up and turned to his two quiet, curious sons.

"Now you can hand me the blanket, Tyler."

His son shoved the plaid comforter toward him, the boy's big eyes wide with wonder—and a keen interest. "Daddy, if she lives, can we keep her?"

Chapter One

Two hours earlier

Icy rain pounded the windshield then fell away like tiny diamonds from a broken necklace.

"It never sleets in South Louisiana!"

Goldie Rios hit her hand on the steering wheel of her compact vehicle, wondering how a perfectly good Saturday in early December had gone from a day of Christmas shopping and a late dinner to driving down this dark, deserted road all by herself.

Nervous and tired, she grabbed the locket she always wore, clutching it briefly with one hand before taking the wheel of the car back with a tight grip. Oh, yes. She remembered with belated bitterness how her day had gone from bad to worse. She'd just dumped another loser of a boyfriend, and right in the middle of a swanky uptown restaurant at the mall near Baton

Rouge. The whole place had gone silent, the only sound Goldie's seething response to Loser Number Five's whining excuses for being seen with another woman one hour before he'd met Goldie for dinner.

The woman was not his sister, his mother, his aunt or his niece. And Goldie was pretty sure she wasn't his grandmother, either, since the cute blonde clung to him in a way that bespoke intimacy rather than family bonds.

She should have listened to her friend Carla—*before* Carla called her from the other end of the mall and told her to casually walk by the pet store. She'd warned Goldie that this one was too smooth, too confident and too good-looking, but Goldie wasn't good at listening to other people's advice. Carla was right. He was in the pet store, buying a cuddly Chihuahua while he cuddled the cute blonde.

Busted.

Goldie watched, horrified and hurt, from behind the Gingerbread House at Santa Claus Lane, while the man she'd been dating for six months kissed another woman. And bought her a dog. He'd never once offered to buy Goldie a dog. In fact, he'd told her he was highly allergic to animals. So after waiting for him to meet her for dinner, Goldie smiled, chatted with him, ordered spaghetti and meatballs and then "accidentally" dumped half her meal onto his lap before telling him that they were finished. It was a standard metaphoric mode of dumping a boyfriend, but now she understood why a lot of women took this route. It made a statement to the world and it made her feel good.

Or at least it had until she'd left the mall in tears.

After driving for an hour in rain that turned to sleet, she'd realized she'd somehow missed the main exit to Viola, Louisiana. Now she was trying to get home through the back way. Bad idea on a night like this and considering she wasn't all that familiar with the roads around here. If she hadn't been so depressed and distracted, she might have thought long and hard about the sanity of taking this remote shortcut. Too late now.

Easing the little car along, Goldie sent up a prayer for safe travels while the radio personality announced yet another road closing due to icy conditions.

"If you're inside, stay there," the perky broadcaster advised. "If you're traveling, stay on the main roads."

Goldie sputtered a reply. "You don't say."

She was not on a main road. And the sleet was getting heavier while the temperature was dipping below freezing. Soon these roads would be slick with ice. Her cell phone rang but since she had both hands glued to the steering wheel and the service out here was questionable at best, Goldie ignored it. Probably Carla calling for details about the breakup. Or maybe Grammy wondering why she wasn't home yet. But she didn't dare talk on the phone and drive in this mess at the same time.

Goldie listened as the "Jingle Bells" ring tone died down, her eyes misting as a wave of loneliness hit her square in her soul. "I guess I'll be alone again this Christmas," she said out loud just to hear herself talking.

No puppy dog for her. And no more snuggling or cuddling with Number Five, either. Five losers in five years. Could her life get any worse? She'd been making the same old mistakes with men since she'd graduated from college and worked in Baton Rouge. Now she'd just have to focus on doing her weekly column on being organized long-distance from Viola while she stayed with her recuperating grandmother through the holidays. In spite of coming here to help Grammy and in hopes of finding some true meaning in her life, Goldie was as confused as ever. Some advice columnist she was. How could she tell other people how to stay focused and organized when she couldn't even keep a man? When would she find what she was looking for—that perfect fit in a relationship?

And why did that matter so much, anyway? She'd never been one to chase after the dream of marriage and family the way some of her single friends did. By Goldie's way of thinking, relationships were highly overrated. So why did she keep dating the wrong men? Maybe so she *could* break up with them and prove her theory? And keep her heart safe in the process?

She held to the steering wheel as she came to a curve, the trees crouching across the road causing her to lose sight of the asphalt. And that's when she hit the patch of slick black ice. The car lurched then shimmied before suddenly changing direction. Screaming, Goldie tried to remember how to steer into the skid, but it was too late. Her car kept slipping and sliding until it went into a careening, screeching turnaround. She looked up, her scream now locked inside her throat, as the car headed right toward the wide trunk of an ancient cypress tree.

The alligator was cooperating. The humans all around the eight-foot reptile, however, were not.

"I want him gone, Rory."

"Me, too. I can't sleep at night, knowing that creature is hibernating right here at my dock. Rory, can you just take him outta here?"

Rory Branagan shivered in his waterproof work boots and his insulated raincoat. His gaze moved from the sedate alligator buried in a self-made bunker of water and mud near the bank to the couple standing in the icy wind. In the yellow glow from the security light, he could see the fear in the couple's eyes. "I understand, Mr. Johnson. But this gator is just doing what alligators do in winter. He's hunkering down for a good long rest."

Alfred Johnson kicked his cowboy boots into the sleet-covered grass near the shallow pond behind his house. "His snout is sticking up out of the water. 'Bout scared my poor wife to death. He coulda grabbed little DeeDee and ate her whole."

"He's not that hungry right now, sir," Rory observed, shaking his head. "And your poodle shouldn't be out here near the water anyway." At least not on a night like this one. And surely these nice people knew that if they lived on a bayou, they were bound to see alligators.

"Good thing I was holding tight to DeeDee," Mrs. Johnson stated, completely ignoring Rory's advice. "Now, it's too cold and wet out here to be arguing. Are you gonna rustle this thing outta here and get him away from my family?"

Rory looked down at the big leathery snout sticking out of the water, thinking Marge Johnson might be petite but she was fiercely protective of the things she loved. That included her family and that barking pile of white fur she called DeeDee. Well, he couldn't blame the woman.

"I think this one here was 'icing' his snout because of the sleet and this frigid water, Mrs. Johnson. He probably wouldn't hurt you as cold as it is out here, since he's not interested in food right now. But if this weather clears and we get some warmer days after Christmas, he could pose a problem."

"So get him," Mr. Johnson instructed, his tone as sharp as the crystals of sleet hitting Rory's broad-brimmed rain hat. "I don't want that gator showing up for Christmas dinner later this month."

"And I don't want him around my grandbabies," Marge insisted, shaking her head, her hair so stiff with hair spray Rory could see tiny ice particles shimmering like a crown on her head. "We've got kids coming home for the holidays and I've got too much to do. I can't be worried about my grandchildren out here by the water."

Rory nodded, steeled himself against a messy job and thought it was nights such as this that made him wish he was in another line of work. But his job as a nuisance hunter for the Louisiana Department of Wildlife and Fisheries paid the bills. And he loved his work on most days. This wasn't a typical day in Louisiana, though. It rarely got this nasty around these parts during the winter. But the sleet was getting heavier by the minute. The forecast for the next couple of days didn't look promising. A rare but sure ice storm was coming, whether Rory liked it or not.

And that old gator was getting real cozy in his nice little cave here on the shore of Mr. Johnson's shallow, marshy pond. If Rory didn't help the poor creature, Mr. Johnson might take matters into his own hands and just shoot the reptile. Rory's conscience couldn't allow that to happen. Nor could his job with the state.

"I'll see what I can do," Rory told Mr. Johnson. "Let me just go to my truck and get my equipment."

"Fair enough," Mr. Johnson replied, satisfied for now at least. "Go on inside, Marge. You're shivering in your wader boots out here, honey."

Rory stomped up the slope toward the driveway, listening to Marge's concerned questions as her husband guided her back to the house. His vibrating cell phone made him stop at the back of the truck.

"What's wrong?" Rory asked into the phone. The

call was from his house and that meant trouble. Having two boys ages six and ten with no mother always meant trouble.

"It's all right."

As always, his mother's voice was calm and firm. "Mom, are you sure?"

"Yes, I'm sure. I just wanted you to know that we're headed over to my house. The boys were getting bored waiting on you and I need to get home anyway to bake cookies for the youth Christmas party at church this Tuesday. Now I have two eager helpers. We're going to make some with cinnamon and sprinkles and lots of icing. That's where we'll be. I offered to let them spend the night but they wanted to be home with you in case this sleet turns to snow. Something about making a gigantic snowman first thing in the morning. You can pick them up when you're done."

Rory smiled at his sons' high hopes. "Are you sure you can make it back in this weather?"

"Rory, I've lived on Branagan Road for over thirty-five years. I think I can drive the mile from your house to mine, son."

"Of course you can." His mother didn't take any bunk and she sure didn't listen to anyone's advice. And that was one of the main reasons Rory loved her.

"Don't worry so much," Frances Branagan declared. "Now let me get on home before it does get worse."

"Thanks," Rory said, appreciation coursing through

his chilled bones. "You're my favorite mom, you know that?"

"I love you, too. Be safe."

He hung up, spoke a prayer of gratitude for his dear patient mother and then set about figuring how to wrestle the unfortunate alligator snoozing down in the pond.

Goldie's feet were cold. She sputtered awake, then groaned as she glanced around. She was in her car, in the dark, on an unfamiliar road. And her head hurt with all the viciousness of two fencers slicing each other to the death, the clanging and banging of her pulse tearing through her temple with each beat of her heart.

She'd wrecked her car. In the ice storm!

Moaning, she pushed at the air bag surrounding her, glad that it had at least saved her from going through the windshield. Then she touched a hand to her head. It was wet and sticky with blood. Weak and disoriented, she groped for the seat belt then after slipping it loose, moaned again when the restraint lifted from her bruised midsection. Automatically reaching for her locket, she clutched it tight. She had to find her phone and call for help.

Her phone, which earlier had been in the seat with her purse, was nowhere to be found now. And she was too dizzy to go digging under the seat.

What should she do? She had to call someone. With great effort, she tried to open the door. After what seemed like hours, the door cringed ajar and a blast of arctic air flowed over Goldie's hot skin. Taking in the crunched front end of her car, she held on to the door as light-headedness washed over her again. She managed to stand, to find her purse. But the phone was lost in the recesses of her shopping bags, notebooks and laptop case. And even if she could find it, she probably wouldn't have very good service.

Goldie gave up on the search and, still woozy and confused, stood and glanced around the woods. She saw a light flickering through the trees.

"A house," she whispered, her prayers raw in her throat. "Maybe someone can help me."

Without giving it much thought other than to find warmth and aid, she slowly made her way along the icy road, her purse clutched to her chest, her head screaming a protest of swirling pain. It was the longest trek of her life and none of the walk made any sense to Goldie. Her brain was fuzzy and her pulse was on fire with a radiating pain. All she could think about was getting out of this freezing sleet.

"Must have a concussion," she voiced to the wind.

When she finally made it to the front door of the house, she was cold, wet and numb with shock. But she knocked and fell against the cool wood, her prayers too hard to voice.

No one came to the door.

So, desperate and beyond caring, she pushed away from the door and continued along the wraparound porch, holding the fat wooden railing until she reached the back of the big farmhouse. Then she fell against the glass-paneled door of the inviting home. Her eyes tried to focus on the Christmas tree sitting in front of the large bay windows and the embers of what looked like a recent fire sparking in the big fireplace.

Goldie wanted that warmth. So she knocked and tried to call out. But no one answered. With one last hope, she jiggled the handle, thinking to herself that she was about to do some serious breaking and entering if she couldn't get any assistance.

And then, the door flew open and Goldie fell through, landing on the cold wide-planked wood of the floor. With a grunt of pain, she crawled to a sitting position then kicked the door shut. Her gaze scanned the big, cozy room and landed for a quick, painful moment on the massive couch across from the still-warm fireplace.

That big brown sofa looked like paradise right now. She's just rest for a minute, then figure out what to do.

Seeing stars that weren't on the tree, Goldie crawled over, pulled herself onto the cushioned pillows and grabbing her beloved locket to hold it close in her hand, and promptly passed out, facedown.

Chapter Two

She had to be dreaming. Goldie sighed in her sleep, glowing warmth moving through her tired bones. She squinted toward the face hovering over her.

The man had dark brown hair and pretty golden eyes but the frown on his face made him look fierce and almost savage. What was he doing in her dream?

Goldie's eyes flew open, pain shooting through her temple like an electrical charge when she tried to sit up. "Where am I?"

"It's okay," the fierce-looking man assured her, pushing her down on the soft pillows. "The ambulance is on its way. You're going to the hospital."

"Hospital?" Goldie tried to sit again but the room started spinning and she felt sick to her stomach. Falling back on the pillows, she asked, "What's wrong with me?"

"You gotta boo-boo."

She closed one eye then slanted the other one toward that tiny voice. A miniature version of Fierce Man stared at her with big, solemn eyes.

"What kind of boo-boo?" Goldie asked, not so sure she wanted an ambulance or an audience. "What happened?"

"You've been in an accident," the man recapped, shooing the little tyke out of the way. "You hit your head."

For a minute, Goldie just lay there staring at her surroundings. This was a nice enough place, but she had no idea how she'd wound up here. "Where am I?"

"This is my house," the man explained. "But don't worry about that right now. Do you remember anything?"

"No." Goldie closed her eyes, hoping that would help the dizziness spiraling through her brain. "I don't know."

"Did you walk here or drive maybe?"

And then she remembered she'd been in a car. Images of that car swirling out of control rushed through her mind. "Yes. Yes. I was in a wreck on the road." She took a deep breath to stop the nausea rising in her stomach. "I lost control and then my head hurt so much. I couldn't find my phone so I got out of the car and I saw the light."

"You broke into our house," came yet another male voice. A different one. This one was more pronounced and angry.

"No, the door was open," Goldie replied, deciding to look at Fierce Man instead of that accusing little person, whoever he was.

The man glanced from Goldie to the boys huddled around her feet. "Did MeeMaw forget to lock the back door?"

The bigger of the two boys shook his head then looked down at the floor. "No, sir. She told me to do it. I was the last one out. I thought I heard it click."

Goldie watched, triumphant because she'd told the truth and now so had the real culprit, as the man's brooding frown changed to a look of complete understanding and forgiveness. "It's okay, son. That old door sticks all the time. I need to see about making it more secure. That happens to me a lot, too."

Goldie thought that was the sweetest thing, the way this man was shouldering the blame for the malfunctioning back door. "I'm glad it wasn't closed," she remarked on a raw spasm of pain, hoping to ease the boy's embarrassment. "I was so cold. And my head hurt a lot."

"So she didn't break in," the tiny one mouthed to the older one, obviously his brother since they looked almost identical. "You need to tell her you're sorry."

"I thought she did," the older one revealed, his hands fisting at his sides. "It looked that way." He didn't say he was sorry.

"Okay, you two. Enough," the man interceded in an authoritative voice. "Step aside and give the nice lady some space."

The boys backed away, their eyes curious and cute.

"I'm so sorry," Goldie apologized to the man. "I didn't mean to pass out on your couch."

"You're hurt," he replied, cutting her the same slack he'd just allowed the boy who'd accidentally left the house unlocked. "Just lie still until we can get you some help."

"How long have I been out?"

"I'm not sure," the man answered. "We got home about fifteen minutes ago. Do you remember anything else?"

She moved her head in an attempt to nod, but the pain stopped her. "My car hit a patch of ice and went sliding right into a tree. A big tree."

"Could have been worse," the man theorized, surveying her. "I think you're okay except for the bang on your head. Must have hit the steering wheel pretty hard."

"It's all fuzzy," she admitted. Then, in spite of her pain and her odd circumstances landing on his couch, she remembered her manners and said, "I'm Goldie Rios."

He smiled at that, sending out a radiant warmth that brought Goldie a sense of comfort and security. "I'm Rory Branagan and these are my sons, Tyler and Sam."

"I'm Tyler," the little one added, grinning.

Sam didn't say anything. He seemed downright sad as he stared at her. Sad and a bit distrustful. How could she blame him? He'd come home to find a strange woman bleeding on his furniture.

"It's good to meet all of you," Goldie responded. "And thanks for being so kind to me."

Rory's soft smile shined again, making Goldie wonder if she might yet be dreaming. This man was a sensitive father. And probably a considerate husband. And for some reason that her hurting brain couldn't quite figure out, that bothered Goldie. Trying to think, she realized she couldn't remember much but the accident. Where had she been? And where was she headed?

The sound of a siren broke Rory's smile and brought Goldie out of her pounding thoughts. He jumped up and went into action while she blinked and closed her eyes. "I think your ride is here." Then he glanced at his sons. "And so is a patrol car. You'll need to give the police a report, nothing to worry about."

Goldie could tell he'd added that last bit for the benefit of his sons, since their eyes grew even wider. The little one showed excitement, but the older boy's eyes held a dark, brooding anger.

If her head hadn't hurt so much, Goldie might have been able to figure that one out. And get to know Not-so-fierce Man a little better. She was certainly content to stay right here in the light of that great smile. But she was in pain, no doubt. And although she wasn't sure if she needed to go to the hospital, she didn't have much choice. Her car was probably totaled and she was too dizzy to stand up. Then, in a clear and concise image in her mind, she remembered her grandmother.

"I need to let Grammy know," she noted. "My grandmother."

"Sure. What's her number?" Rory replied. "I'll call her right now."

Goldie rattled off the numbers, glad her brain was beginning to cooperate. "Her name is Ruth Rios."

Rory let out a chuckle. "You don't say? I should have made the connection when you told me your name. I know Miss Ruth. She goes to my church. So you're her granddaughter?"

Goldie nodded. "I just came here a few weeks ago to help her out. She's been recovering from hip surgery."

"Yeah, we heard that and since she hasn't been to church in a while... I'm sure sorry." He gave her an apologetic look. "I should have gone by to see her."

"She's doing better," Goldie informed him. "But I know she's worried since I'm not home yet. I was supposed to be there hours ago."

"I'll call her, I promise," Rory reiterated as the paramedics knocked on the door, followed by one of the three police officers serving Viola.

Goldie nodded, her mind whirling with pain and confusion. "Don't let her get out in this weather. She doesn't need to come to the hospital." After that, she didn't get much of a chance to say anything else to Rory. She was too busy being examined and questioned, both of which left her tired and even more confused.

The paramedics checked her vitals, asked her all the pertinent questions and concluded yes, she might have a mild concussion. And the officer seemed satisfied that she'd been in a one-car accident and that she hadn't been drinking. He and Rory both assured her they'd have the car towed. So she was off to the hospital.

"I appreciate your help," Goldie mumbled to Rory as she was lifted up and hustled onto the waiting gurney.

"Don't worry about that," Rory commented, following her stretcher out into the chilly night. "Take care, Goldie."

"Thanks," she mumbled again as the ambulance doors shut. She could just make out his image as he talked to the police officer.

But as she lay there with two efficient paramedics fussing over her, Goldie wondered if she'd ever see Rory Branagan again.

Doubtful, since she wouldn't be staying here in Viola much longer now that Grammy was better. And double doubtful since she didn't attend church with Grammy.

Or at least, she hadn't yet.

The next morning, Goldie hung up the phone by her hospital bed to find Rory standing in the door of her room, holding a huge poinsettia in a green pot.

"Uh, hi," he said, the big red and green plant blocking his face. "The nurse said I could come in."

Goldie grinned then motioned to him. "Hi, yourself. I just talked to Grammy. She said you were so nice last night, calling her and keeping her informed. And that you wouldn't let her get out in the weather even to come visit me."

He lifted his chin in a quick nod. "She was pretty stubborn about doing just that, but I called her neighbor and asked her to sit with your grandmother. Then I contacted the hospital to check on you. Only, they didn't want to give me any information. So I phoned your grandmother again and explained it to her, since she was your next of kin." He laughed, took a breath then asked, "So how are you?"

"I'm fine," Goldie reported, her heart doing an odd little dance as he set down the plant and came closer. "You didn't have to go to all that trouble."

"No trouble. Me and Miss Ruth go back a long way. I once rescued an armadillo out of her backyard."

"Excuse me?" Goldie reclined against her pillows, taking in his crisp plaid flannel shirt and sturdy jeans. She didn't think it was possible that he still looked so handsome, even in the glaring morning light, but he did.

"I work for the Department of Wildlife and Fisheries as a nuisance hunter. I get calls to trap wild animals, anything from armadillos and snakes to alligators and even the occasional black bear."

"You're kidding?"

He looked downright sheepish. "No, that's my job."

"Isn't that sorta dangerous?"

He grinned again. "Not as dangerous as forcing myself to come to the hospital in an ice storm to check on you. And mind you, it wasn't the storm that scared me."

He did seem a bit uncomfortable. He fidgeted with the water jar and rearranged her drinking cup. And Goldie's impish nature clicked on. "What, you don't like hospitals?"

"That and…I'm a bit rusty on talking to women."

She filed that comment away to study more closely later. He had two little boys so he was obviously a happily married man. Disappointing but comforting in a strange way. He looked like the kind of man who belonged in a family.

Nobody liked hospitals but the expression in his eyes told her maybe he'd had some firsthand experience with this kind of thing. Maybe she'd ask him about that, too, but right now, she only wanted to put him at ease. "I'm easy to talk to on most days and I really like the flower."

"It was the only thing I could find at the superstore on the highway."

"It's pretty, but again, you didn't have to come see me."

"I promised Miss Ruth." He shrugged. "And I wanted to make sure you were all right."

Goldie stared at the plant. "I have a slight concussion, but they're releasing me this afternoon. I just have to rest for the weekend and take over-the-counter pain reliever. No ibuprofen though, since it can cause some sort of bleeding—doctor's orders." She motioned to a paper on the bedside table. "I have a whole list of instructions on all the things to watch for after a concussion." And she wondered if one of those things was a rapid pulse, and if Rory or her head injury was the cause of that symptom.

"So, what about your confusion and memory loss?"

She slanted her throbbing head. "I still can't quite remember much more about the accident or what I was doing most of yesterday, but I'm okay. The doctor said I might not ever remember all of it. He just warned me of dizziness and confusion at times. But hey, I'm that way on a good day."

He fingered one of the vivid red poinsettia leaves. "Your car was full of shopping bags."

"You've seen my car?"

"I had it towed, remember?" He seemed embarrassed. "I guess you don't. It's at a nearby garage. But I got all the stuff out of it. It's in my car right now. I can take it by your grandmother's if you want me to."

Goldie shook her head. "You're amazing. What's the catch?"

"Excuse me?" he asked, echoing her earlier words to him. "What catch?"

She shrugged, wincing at her sore muscles. "You just seem too good to be true."

He lowered his head. When he looked back up, his eyes were dark with some unspoken emotion. "Oh, I'm not, trust me. I just walked across the woods last night with the policeman to check on your car and then I notified a friend who owns a body shop to tow it. After you file your insurance report and get the go-ahead, he'll give you a good estimate—that is if you want him to fix the car."

Goldie decided not to question why he deflected the compliment. "Can it be fixed?"

"Maybe." He stood quietly and then said, "I hope I didn't overstep—having him pick up the car."

Goldie shook her head. "No, not at all. I just didn't need this to happen right now. I'm here to help Grammy and I depend on my car to get me around. Just one more thing to deal with."

He inclined his head in understanding. "Maybe you can rent a car or drive your grandmother's."

Goldie laughed. "Her car is ancient but it does move, barely. Grammy says it has one speed—slow."

His smile was back. "I see you have her sense of humor."

"Keeps me sane."

He seemed amused then said, "Well, I guess I'd better get back to the house. I left my sons with my mother—again. That poor woman never gets a break." His smile was indulgent. "We made two snowmen—one in our yard and one in hers."

She looked out the window. "Did it snow last night?"

"Yeah, a pretty good dusting. The ground is covered white and we were able to get two passable snowmen."

"Are the roads okay, then?"

"The roads are fine now. I had to be careful driving into town, but the sun melted most of the ice. However, we could have another round tomorrow." He turned toward the door then whirled. "Hey, do you need a ride home?"

Goldie didn't know how to respond. This man seemed to know what she needed even before she voiced it. That was very disconcerting to a woman who was used to being independent and confident and…alone. "I hadn't thought about that. I sure don't want Grammy trying to find someone to drive me, even if the roads are clear."

"I can take you right now."

He really was a sweet man. "I haven't been released yet. The doctor said later today."

"I'll come back and take you home, then," he confirmed, holding up a hand when she tried to protest. "I just have to help the boys do some things around our place. We have a small herd of cows and they need checking on and we all have chores to do, but they can stay with my mom while I take you to your grandmother's house."

"I don't want to impose."

"I insist. Your grandmother's worried about you and I don't mind. I'll call her."

"I can call Grammy," Goldie asserted. "I'll tell her you're bringing me home. They said midafternoon, after I see the doctor one more time and he signs my release."

"So, I'll be back around three."

Goldie had to ask. "You said your mother watches the boys a lot? Does your wife work?" And where had his wife been last night?

"I don't have a wife," he corrected, the light going out of his eyes. "She...died a few years ago."

Wishing she'd learn to keep her curiosity to herself, Goldie looked down at her hands. That probably explained his aversion to hospitals. "I'm so sorry."

He didn't comment. He just nodded his head again in a silent acknowledgment. "I'll see you at three."

"Okay. Thanks again, Rory. For everything."

He waved goodbye then shut the door.

"Nice going, Goldie," she whispered to herself. If her head hadn't been so sore, she would have hit her forehead in disgust. Why was she accident-prone with herself and her mouth?

Instead, Goldie closed her eyes and remembered the homeyness of Rory's rambling farmhouse, the cute grins of his two little boys—wait, the cute grin of the youngest of his two boys, at least—and the way Rory's eyes crinkled when he smiled. And she imagined the kind of woman who'd once been a part of that lovely picture. The kind of woman who baked cookies, kept the house neat and played kick ball with the boys in the backyard. A loving, caring, motherly type woman.

And she reminded herself she was not that kind of woman even if she did have a compulsion toward being organized. Besides, she'd come here to help her grandmother, not get involved with yet another male even if this one seemed to actually understand the meaning of the words *trust* and *commitment*. In spite of her accident and her fuzzy memories, she somehow knew she had a very good reason for not wanting a man in her life—no matter how kind Rory Branagan had been to her and how much her heart was telling her that this man just might be different from all the rest.

Chapter Three

Her locket was missing.

Frantic, Goldie searched all around her bed and the bedside table, then buzzed for a nurse. She glanced at the clock. It was almost time for Rory to come and take her home, but she couldn't leave without her locket. When the bubbly RN rushed into her room, Goldie was just about out of the bed.

"Don't try to get up by yourself," the nurse objected, holding Goldie's arm. "Do you need a bathroom break?"

"No, I…I can't find my locket," Goldie replied, willing herself not to cry. "It's on a gold chain—it's a filigree-etched square with a porcelain picture of a Louisiana iris and a tiny yellow butterfly. Somebody must have taken it off me when they brought me in."

The nurse opened drawers and went through the nearby closet. "Here's the bag that came with your personal belongings. Want me to check inside? It might be in your purse."

Goldie nodded. "If you don't mind."

She watched closely as the nurse searched her leather purse then rummaged through Goldie's clothes from last night. "I don't see anything like that, honey. Maybe you gave the locket to someone for safekeeping before you came here?"

"No," Goldie replied, trying to think. Had Rory removed the locket last night? Or had she lost it? She couldn't remember. What if someone had taken it? She'd never forgive herself if something had happened to it.

"Just relax and I'll ask at the desk," the nurse advised, trying to reassure her as she handed Goldie her belongings.

Goldie bobbed her head. "Ask everyone. I have to find it. It's very old and has a lot of sentimental value."

"Okay." The nurse walked toward the door. "I'll see what I can do, but you know the hospital isn't—"

"I know—not responsible for the loss of valuables," Goldie repeated. "I understand."

But she wanted her necklace back. She had to find it. So she waited for the nurse to leave, then she carefully got up to search on her own. She made it to the end of the bed but she stood up too quickly. Her pulse quickened as blood rushed from her head and made her dizzy.

And that's when Rory walked in and grabbed her just as she reached for the bed for support.

* * *

"Hey, hey," Rory urged, guiding Goldie back to the bed. "Where you going, sunshine?"

"My locket," Goldie explained, squeezing her eyes shut to stop the stars flashing through her brain. "I…I think I lost it."

He gazed down at her. She looked so young and innocent, lying there devoid of makeup. Her hair wasn't exactly blond, more burnished and gold than a true blond. It shimmered like silky threads against her cheeks while the square patch of gauze just over her hairline shined starkly white. The frown on her face only made her look more like a lost little girl than a determined woman.

"I remember your locket. You were wearing it last night. At least, I saw it when I turned you over on the couch."

"I was?" She sat up again. "Maybe I lost it at your house."

"I'll look when I get home," he said. Because this woman had disrupted his life to the point that he was worried about her *and* what she meant to him as a man, he asked, "So what's the deal with that pretty locket, anyway?"

She looked away, toward the window. "My daddy gave it to me before he went to war during Desert Storm. It has a picture of me and him inside it. He never made it home."

"Oh, wow." Rory felt bad for being so nosy. "I'm

sure sorry to hear that. No wonder it means so much to you."

"It does and it's very old. It belonged to his great-great-grandmother. And my grandmother gave it to him to give to me on my twelfth birthday. It's kind of a tradition in our family. Grammy says good things happen to the women who wear that locket. So far, that hasn't exactly been the case with me."

Rory hadn't pegged her for being traditional nor for feeling sorry for herself, but under the circumstances, he could certainly understand why she looked so down. And he could sympathize with her need to find the piece of jewelry. "I'll look over the house and in the yard, too. I'll get the boys to help."

"I'd appreciate that." She stared at the ceiling. "I've made such a mess of things. Wrecking my car, losing my necklace. I need to get my life together somehow."

Rory could tell she was fighting back tears. "Listen, your car might be fixable and…well, we'll probably find your locket. Just be glad you're okay. That wreck could have been much worse."

She looked over at him, her smile bittersweet. "I guess I am acting a little over-the-top. And you're right. I'm still here and Grammy needs me. It's just that was one of the few things my daddy ever gave me. My parents were divorced so I didn't get to see him much."

"That's a shame," Rory replied. "I'm blessed that

my parents had a great marriage. My mom's a widow now, but I had a pretty good childhood. Nothing major—just lots of good memories."

She smiled again. "Yes, you are blessed. I've never had that. We transferred all over while my dad was alive and in the army, then my mother moved us around a lot after the divorce. Grammy was the one who kept me grounded and safe, even if she and my mother don't always see eye to eye."

"And where's your mother now? Should I call her?"

She shook her head. "No. That's okay. I'll give her an update when she checks on us. She's traveling overseas, one of those long tours with a bunch of her friends—a big Christmas extravaganza. Angela likes to travel and she rarely calls home."

Rory thought her daughter did not like that arrangement. In spite of her pretty curls and her soft smile, he sensed loneliness in Goldie. And he wondered how long she'd been searching for a safe place to lay her head. "Hey, let's get you home to your grandmother. She's told me she's got a big pot of homemade chicken soup simmering on the stove just for you. And fresh-baked corn bread to go with it."

"Grammy's answer to anything is chicken soup," Goldie said. "And she makes the best. She puts homemade dumplings in there."

"I take it you like her cooking," Rory replied, grinning.

"I like food, period." She laughed then grimaced.

"And if I stay with her much longer, I won't be able to fit into any of my clothes."

Rory thought Goldie looked just perfect, but he refrained from making such a flirtatious comment since they didn't really know each other. Yet.

Then he told himself not to even think along those lines. He had enough to keep him busy, what with the boys, his mother and his work and, well, a man got lonely just like a woman did, he reasoned.

But he didn't need to think about that right now.

"Has the doctor been by?" he asked, suddenly ready to get out of here.

Goldie waved toward the hallway. "Yes. I'm sorry, I guess you're ready. I was waiting on the nurse. She's checking around for my locket."

"Oh, okay." He tapped his knuckles on the food tray. "Got everything else together?"

"Yes. One of Grammy's friends brought me this change of clothes. I sent your poinsettia home with her."

He noticed she was wearing a sweater and some wide-legged sweatpants. "I could have brought that. I didn't even think about clothes."

"You've done more than enough," Goldie said. "Besides, I think Grammy sent Phyllis to check on me and bring back a thorough report. And if I know my grandmother and Phyllis, they probably tag-teamed my doctor to get the whole story on my injuries."

"Are you sure you're up to going home?"

"Oh, yes, I'm ready to get into my own bed." She lifted up. "Let's go to the desk and see where that nurse is."

Rory helped her. "Are you still dizzy?"

"No. I think I just got up too quickly before. And we're not telling the nurse about that little episode. It wasn't the awful dizziness I had after the wreck. I have work to do and I need to get back to it."

"Oh, I don't think you need to worry about work. It's the weekend."

"I have a deadline," she explained. "I write a syndicated advice column. It's mostly about organizing your house and keeping your life straight—something I haven't been doing lately. And I'm already pushing things with my boss by working long distance."

Rory gained a new insight. "A column? That's interesting."

"Not as interesting as being a nuisance hunter," she retorted, standing on wobbly legs.

Rory laughed at that. "We'll have to compare notes on that some time. I could use tips on organization and keeping things straight and orderly in my life, that's for sure."

"And I've always wanted to track down an alligator and wrestle it until I can tie its mouth shut," she teased.

Rory got a picture of this petite woman holding down a ten-foot reptile. It made him smile.

"Don't think I can do it?" she asked as they made it out of her room.

"I have no doubt," he replied, not willing to argue the point with an injured woman.

"And I think you'd be pretty good at doling out advice," she replied. "At least, I think women would listen to you no matter what you say. They'd follow your advice based on your smile alone."

That made him take notice. Giving her the best smile he could muster, he prompted, "So, you like my smile, huh?"

She laughed, a soft pink flush coloring her cheeks. "I do when I'm not seeing two of you."

"Are you okay?"

"I'm fine. I just wish I hadn't lost my locket. Let's get out of here, though, so you don't have to wait."

"Not so fast, young lady."

They turned to find her doctor and the nurse who'd been in her room trailing them down the hallway. "You need to be in this. Standard hospital policy."

Goldie glared at the wheelchair. "Oh, all right." Settling herself into the chair, she turned to the nurse. "Did you find my locket?"

"I'm afraid not, honey," the nurse replied. "I'm sorry. Everything that came in with you should be in that bag the paramedics put your personal things in."

Goldie clutched her purse and the plastic bag labeled with her name. "Maybe somebody dropped it in here and we just didn't see it. It could be in the pocket of the jeans I was wearing yesterday."

"We'll look when we get you home," Rory suggested, hoping to distract her from tossing out the contents of her purse and the bag right here. Or refusing to get home to some rest. She looked so upset, he wondered if she shouldn't stay in the hospital another night.

She didn't answer. She was too busy digging around in the deep recesses of her big leather purse, pulling out various labeled little sacks of all sorts. She had a bag for everything inside that larger bag. "I sure hope I can find it."

"We'll keep looking," the nurse said, waving to them.

When they got outside, Goldie had that lost expression on her face again.

"They won't find it," she said. "Somebody probably stole it. It's pretty valuable, considering how old it is. But I don't care about how much money it can bring. I just want it back."

Rory could understand her frustrations. And her disappointment. He hoped he could find that locket for Goldie, but he had his doubts, too. Even though it hadn't snowed more than a couple of inches last night, a piece of jewelry could easily become lost in all the mush. He'd have to go over the yard and house with an eagle eye.

After getting Goldie into his car, Rory started out of the parking lot and onto the main highway. "So where did you live when you're not in Viola?"

"Baton Rouge," she answered, her gaze on the road. "Wow, I see patches of snow in the trees. And the ground is still covered. It's so beautiful even if it does hurt my eyes."

"It was pretty cold last night. Some of that could freeze up again later." Trying to get to know her better, he continued, "And what did you do in Baton Rouge? I mean, how long have you been writing the column?"

"Since college," she replied. Then she turned to look at him. "I went to school at LSU and got a degree in communication. I wasn't sure what I wanted to do. I had written a column for a school newspaper and that experience gave me a chance to write a column for a paper in Baton Rouge. Because my most popular columns were on organization and how to get your life on track, I got promoted to the lifestyles section and after three years, the column became regionally syndicated. But I do feature articles, advertorials and fillers, too. I don't make a lot of money, but I enjoy my work. I've always been highly organized so it's nice to use those skills in my job."

"Kind of like that woman on television my mother likes so much. I can't remember her name but she does a cooking show."

Goldie knew of the woman in question. "No, more like a Southern version of the modern woman—you know, busy, stressed, working all the time both in the home and out of the home and needing to fold the laundry and cook a decent meal then finish studying a business report. I interview a lot of women to get the best tips."

"My wife was like that," he said, then wished he hadn't mentioned Rachel. He didn't like to talk about her.

Goldie gave him a nod. "Your home reflects that. I'm impressed that it was so neat."

He shrugged. "My mom was over last night, cleaning for me. You should have seen it when I left yesterday morning."

"Oh, your mother. Well, I'm sure she loves helping out."

"She's been a blessing…since…since Rachel died. She's a big help with the house and the boys. I guess that works two ways since we lost my dad a year ago. She likes the company."

"I'm sorry about your wife and your dad." Goldie didn't say anything else. She just stared out at the road ahead.

Thinking his past tragedies were sure a downer and not the best approach to impressing a woman, Rory was glad when they pulled up to her grandmother's tiny brick house. He didn't need to worry about impressing a woman, anyway. "I'll help you get in and say hi to your grandmother."

Goldie waited for him to come around the car then slowly lifted herself out to face him. "I might as well warn you, Rory. She's gonna want you to stay and eat. But you don't have to. That is, unless you want to, I mean."

Rory smiled down at her, thinking soup and corn

bread was mighty tempting right now. Especially if he'd get to sit across the table from Goldie.

Then he remembered his boys waiting at his mother's house and he thought about Rachel, how much he still missed her, and he wondered why he was even thinking about another woman.

"I'd better get on home," he told Goldie as he helped her up the two stone steps to the porch.

"Nonsense, Rory Branagan," came the sweet but firm voice from inside the open door. Ruth stood there holding on to a walker. "After all you've done for Goldie, the least we can do is give you a good meal. Now come on in here and have some dinner. I insist."

Rory looked from Goldie's "I told you so" grin to Ruth Rios's twinkling eyes and realized he was trapped between longing and duty. And that was not a good place for a man.

Or at least he didn't think it was.

But he went into the house and shut the door anyway.

Chapter Four

"More coconut pie, Rory?"

"No, ma'am." Rory glanced over at Goldie, shot her a smile then looked back at her grandmother. "I don't think I can eat another bite. And I really need to head on home."

The man was fidgety. Goldie had noticed that earlier today in the hospital, only then she'd chalked it up to his memories of his wife's death. But now, he just seemed like a caged animal wanting out. Did she make him that nervous? Or was he just used to being outside, cornering some varmint instead of sitting with two women as if he were a member of the garden club?

"Grammy, you know Rory has two boys. And they're probably wondering where their daddy is."

"'Course I know all about his boys," Ruth replied, pursing her lips in that Grammy way. "I've taught both of them in Sunday school. Adorable."

Rory laughed at that. He had a deep laugh. A steady laugh. Goldie liked the sound of it.

"I wouldn't exactly call them adorable now. They can be a handful, that's for sure. Which is why I'd better relieve my mom. She's had them for two days in a row."

"Do you go out a lot?" Grammy asked, her tone as innocent as the fresh snow still outside.

Rory looked shocked then shook his head. "No, not on dates or stuff like that. I had a call last night from the Johnsons. They spotted an old gator snoozing under the icy water near their dock. Mrs. Johnson wasn't happy."

"I reckon not," Grammy agreed, clearly fascinated. "How'd you catch him?"

Rory tapped his fingers on the table, no doubt ready to be on the road and away from two curious females. "Well, I didn't want to have to kill him, so I just put on my waders and went in and roped him."

"You hear that, Goldie? Roped an alligator, all by himself. You ever heard of such?"

Goldie gave Rory an apologetic smile. "Can't say that I have, Grammy. I'd be afraid I'd lose an arm or leg, going into water with an alligator."

Rory shook his head. "He was hibernating. An easy catch. I loaded him up and tagged him—we like to keep records on how many we catch and release."

"So you did release him?" Goldie repeated, suddenly as fascinated as her grandmother.

"We try to release as many as we can. But sometimes, we have to shoot 'em."

"That's too bad," Goldie said, imagining this soft-spoken man shooting to kill. He might be soft-spoken right now but she could picture him as an expert hunter. Why did that make a little shiver slink down her backbone?

"She never did like to see any of God's creatures hurt or dying," Ruth murmured, her hand over her mouth in a mock whisper. "She'd bring home every stray out there if I let her."

Goldie couldn't argue with that. "She's right. I love animals. But I've never been in one spot long enough to even have a gerbil, let alone a dog or cat."

"She's kind of a nomad," Grammy offered up. "A wandering soul."

"What she means," Goldie interpreted, wishing her grandmother wouldn't talk about her personal inadequacies so much, "is that I can't seem to settle down."

"Well, you've been all over," Grammy argued, pouring Rory a second cup of coffee with automatic sweetness. "Traveled all over Europe and the whole United States, this one."

Goldie nodded. "That's why I like working at the paper. I can go anywhere I want and still get my column submitted on time. Plus, I pick up ideas and suggestions for my readers when I travel and with technology, it's fairly easy to do feature stories on the road, too."

Rory was now the one who seemed fascinated. "I've rarely left Louisiana. Is it fun, traveling around all the time?"

Goldie felt the scrutiny of his gaze. The man's job sure suited him. He looked like he could track down the wildest of animals.

"It...uh...can be fun, yes. But Grammy's exaggerating. My parents moved me around a lot when I was growing up, so that's what I'm used to. Then I did some traveling on my own after high school and college. Just summer tours." Sending her grandmother a warning glance, she added, "But I'm here in good ol' Viola for a while."

"And I'm grateful to have her," Grammy acknowledged. "She's taken good care of her old grandma, let me tell you. And even though I'm up and around, using my walker, she insists on staying through Christmas. So we have a few more weeks with her."

"That should be a blessing for you, Miss Ruth." Rory got up. "I hate to leave such good company, ladies, but I have to get home." He looked down at Goldie. "I'm glad you're okay and I'll search for your locket the minute I get home."

Grammy's gaze centered on Goldie's neck. "You lost your locket, honey?"

"I've misplaced it, yes," Goldie echoed, her smile waning. "I hope I dropped it at Rory's house last night. I've explained to him how much it means to me."

Grammy didn't seem too concerned. She patted Goldie's hand. "Well, lockets can be replaced. You can't."

Goldie pushed the cobwebs of regret out of her

mind, deciding to think positively. With a wry grin, she said, "I am one of a kind."

Grammy laughed at that. "You sure are."

Rory just stood there, smiling his soft smile, his eyes so tigerlike, Goldie could almost feel sorry for alligators and armadillos.

"I'll walk you out," she said, getting up. Glad the dizziness wasn't back, she slowly made her way around the antique mahogany dining table.

"Don't overdo it now," Grammy warned, but Goldie caught the gleam in her grandmother's eyes.

Rory took her arm. "You don't have to see me to the door. It's cold out there."

"I just wanted to thank you again, for all you've done," Goldie said, a rare shyness taking over her tongue.

"Not a problem. Just be careful next time an ice storm hits, okay?"

"That might not happen again in a long time," she replied, being reasonable. "But that's the way things go for me—the first ice storm in Louisiana in years and I wind up on the worst road in the state."

"Well, if it does happen again and you find yourself out near Branagan Road, you know where I live."

A rush of something warm and satisfying moved down Goldie's spine. "Yes, I sure do."

"I'll call you if I find the necklace," he said, throwing up a hand in goodbye.

"Okay."

She shut the door against the cold wind, bright red felt Christmas bows lifting out from the wreath she'd made to hang there, and she wondered if she'd ever see her necklace again.

And if she'd ever see this man again.

He planned on seeing her again.

Rory wasn't sure if it was the chicken soup or the coconut pie or the blondish curls, but somewhere during the hour or so he'd spent with Goldie and her grandmother, he'd decided he'd like to get to know Goldie Rios a little better. Only he wasn't so sure how to go about that.

I'm rusty on this stuff, Lord, he thought, his prayers as scattered as the frigid wind. He hadn't considered dating anyone since Rachel's death. In fact, he'd believed that to be an insult to his wife's memory. And to her love for him and their boys.

But maybe he'd been wrong about that. Maybe the boys needed a mother's touch. His own mother was a pretty terrific substitute and the boys loved her dearly, but well, a man needed a wife. Especially a man trying to raise two active sons. Telling himself to slow down, Rory pushed contemplations of finding a wife out of his mind. That would be wrong—to automatically think of Goldie in those terms when he'd only just met the woman.

Right now, he wouldn't think beyond getting to know her. One day at a time, he reminded himself.

After all, she was the first woman who'd even made him stop to consider dating again. And maybe he was just caught up in the whole thing—finding her on his couch, hurt and frightened, seeing that lost expression in her eyes when she told him about her locket and watching her wince as her grandmother bragged on her, going into detail about her life.

Goldie was obviously a smart, capable woman.

But from the look of things, she wasn't anywhere near settling down to one man. One man with two rambunctious children.

"I'd better find that locket and get it back to her before I do something really dumb," Rory said to himself.

Like ask her out on a date or something.

But that urge might be tougher to control than wrestling a gator had ever been.

"Grammy, I know that look," Goldie said after Rory had left. "You're up to matchmaking, aren't you?"

"The thought never crossed my mind," Ruth teased, her smile causing her dimples to deepen. "But you have to admit, Rory is a fine-looking man. And a good, solid Christian, too."

"I don't doubt that," Goldie replied. "He does seem like a good person."

"And nice-looking, right?"

"Can't fault him there, either."

"And he is single and lonely, bless his heart."

"Yes, bless his heart," Goldie echoed. "But, Grams, you know I won't be here that long now that you're better. I have to go back to Baton Rouge after Christmas."

Grammy shook her head, her silver curls glistening even if they were too clipped to move. "You know, you don't have to go back to that big city. You could stay here a while longer. You said so yourself—you can do your work from anywhere."

Goldie put the rest of the pie in the refrigerator. "Yes, I did say that. But I have an apartment in Baton Rouge and I have friends there. And I do have to show up at the paper for editorial meetings and planning sessions and such. My boss has been very kind in allowing me to work from here but he won't let that go on forever."

Ruth slapped the lid on the plastic container of leftover soup. "Of course you have to get back one day, darlin'. But it's been so nice having you here with me. Not that I need you to hover over me, but you do make for pleasant company."

Goldie counted to ten, telling herself not to let that grandmotherly guilt get her all confused. "I love your company, too. And that's why I agreed to stay through the rest of December. But come January one, I'm going home."

"You're too tough," Ruth said. "Too stubborn and too tough. Men don't always appreciate those qualities in a woman."

"I'm not looking for a man," Goldie retorted, stung

by her grandmother's words. "Now, are we going to watch that classic movie I rented the other day, or are you tired?"

"You're the one who just came home from the hospital," Ruth proclaimed in a gentle tone. "How're you feeling?"

"I feel okay," Goldie admitted. "No dizziness and just a few fuzzy memories."

"Oh, don't forget to call your friend back," Grammy said, heading for the small den at the front of the house. "She was really worried about you, especially since you and what's-his-name had a bad fight."

Goldie's eyes widened as memories came floating down on her like snowflakes. She'd been at the mall, eating dinner with what's-his-name. The same one who'd just bought a puppy for another woman—in the same mall. Some things weren't worth remembering. "I'll call Carla, then start the movie," she said.

But she didn't reach for the phone right away. Instead, she stood there looking out the kitchen window, listening to her grandmother's wind chimes hanging on the small back porch playing a tune in the night breeze. The yard was illuminated by a bright yellow security light and the trees danced and swayed, soft white flakes of leftover snow shivering to the ground with each blast of wind. It had snowed in southern Louisiana.

Nothing normal had happened to her over this last

weekend. Ice. Snow. Another breakup—okay, that was normal. Then the car wreck. And she'd wound up in a stranger's house, hurt and confused. A stranger who'd turned out to be a nice man with two cute kids. What were the odds of that happening? And to her, of all people?

And to top it off, she's lost the one possession she treasured above anything else, her golden locket. Good things were supposed to happen with that locket, but so far Goldie could only count her "good things" on one hand. While she could count her not-so-good relationships breaking up on the other hand.

I've had too many disappointing tries at finding a soul mate, Lord. So I won't get my hopes up again.

She might have lost her precious locket to Rory Branagan. But she would not lose her heart.

Rory walked up the path to his mother's rambling ranch-style house, missing his dad. It was times such as these he'd go into his dad's big workshop out back and have a man-to-man discussion on doing the right thing. However, he wasn't here anymore. But Rory could talk to God, asking for strength and guidance, and he could talk to his mom on most subjects. At least he had his faith to get him through the rough spots.

And he was in a rough spot tonight, for sure.

Of all the houses, how'd she wind up in mine?

He'd been limping along, getting things done and taking care of his boys. He'd managed to restart his life after Rachel had died. For his boys' sake he'd prayed for God to ease the anger and the bitterness of his wife's senseless death, had even tried to forgive the person who'd taken her life. But not once in the last long months had he ever asked God to send him a replacement. Because no one could replace Rachel.

And it hurt him to even think in those terms.

But he still couldn't get Goldie Rios out of his mind.

"You gonna turn into an icicle, standing out there on the steps, son."

Rory looked around to find his mother at the door, her shawl clasped around her shoulders. "Hey, Mom. Sorry I'm so late—again."

"Get in here," Frances ordered, her smile indulgent and full of a mother's love.

Rory knocked the mud and dirty snow off his boots. "Where are the boys?"

"In the back den, watching one of those children's movies you keep me supplied with. We played some games, had some chili for dinner and now they're quiet and absorbed in watching talking animals going on all kinds of adventures."

He shut the door then took off his down jacket. "Mom, am I taking advantage of your good graces?"

Frances pulled her shawl more tightly around her shoulders. "Rory, haven't we had this conversation before? You know how I feel about those two. I don't mind helping out."

"But you have a life," he countered, guilt weighing at him. "I could find a sitter occasionally."

"Don't you dare," Frances replied, motioning to the kitchen. "C'mon. I just made hot chocolate."

Rory followed her into the neat, whitewashed room. He'd helped his father redo the cabinets and tile in this kitchen. "Maybe I should spend more time with them."

"That can't hurt," Frances reflected, handing him a mug of the steaming chocolate milk. "Sam acts out now and then."

"Has he been giving you trouble?"

"Nothing I can't handle," Frances replied. "He gets a little smart-alecky at times but I think he just misses his mother. And...he's growing up so fast."

"Then I do need to spend more time with them."

"You have to work, son. And I don't mind being the disciplinarian, as long as I have your permission on that."

"You know you do. But I'm gonna make sure I get home on time—as many days as I can. And I'll do more with them on the weekends. We've got soccer and baseball again in the spring at least."

"That's good, but your job is unpredictable. Just keep doing the best you can and God will take care of the rest."

Rory looked around the corner toward the den where Sam and Tyler lay curled in the sleeping bags Frances kept here just for them. He loved his boys with all his heart and each time he looked at them, he missed their mother.

"What's wrong, anyway?" Frances asked. Then she put a hand to her throat. "Is it this woman? The girl you found in your house last night?"

Rory could never hide anything from his mother. He shrugged. "She sure did shake up my normal routine."

"I'll say. It was mighty nice of you to give her a ride home from the hospital."

"I did it for Miss Ruth. You know she's been down with hip replacement surgery. Goldie's staying with her until she's well again."

Frances looked doubtful. "That sounds like a nice gesture but surely this girl won't be around much longer, right?"

Rory knew what his mother was saying. Goldie would go back to Baton Rouge soon and therefore, he had no business getting involved with her. "I think she's staying through the holidays."

Frances put down her empty cup. "Hmm. Holidays have a way of making everything look so lovely, don't they?"

Then she turned and headed into the den, leaving her son to wonder what in the world she was talking about. Did his mother think he was going to have some holiday fling then just go back to life as usual once the new year came?

Didn't she know he wasn't that kind of man?

Yes, she did. But she didn't know what kind of

woman Goldie Rios was and that was why she'd made such a pointed statement to him.

And she might be right. Because Rory knew that just like the fresh snow that had fallen last night, things could turn ugly come the light of day. And he had his boys to protect.

No time to even consider getting to know Goldie Rios even though he'd been thinking of doing that exact thing.

He'd just search for her locket and leave it at that. It was the best thing to do, all the way around.

Chapter Five

Dear Goldie:

How do I get rid of the clutter in my life? My house is a wreck and so is my love life. I can't help but wonder if the two are connected—Shipwrecked in Serepta

A few days later, Goldie stared at the e-mail question, thinking she could use some advice on that subject herself. While her topics mostly concentrated on rearranging furniture and adding plants and flowers to make a room "pop," her readers sometimes threw her a curve ball by combining messiness in their homes with messiness in their personal lives. And this was one such question.

"Talk about timing."

Well, she owed this reader an answer and she also owed her publisher a column for this week. And her blog needed updating. So she'd better come up with a concrete, logical answer. Did she dare tell her readers about her accident and her blow to the head? And that she'd been rescued by a wonderful man but she was too afraid to flirt with him and get to know him?

"Maybe later," she said out loud. She didn't want to overload her loyal followers with the shaky details of her own troubles. She'd just answer this question to the best of her abilities, based on her own instincts and tons of research from experts.

She'd keyed in "Dear Shipwrecked" when a knock came at her bedroom door.

"Yes?" Knowing it was her grandmother, Goldie tried to sound upbeat. Grams didn't like downers or whiners.

"Are you going to church with me? It's Wednesday-night dinner and devotions."

"No, Grams. I have a deadline." And since she'd only had one quick phone call from Rory, telling her he hadn't found her locket anywhere on his property, Goldie couldn't even use that excuse for trying to see him at church. Besides, that would be just plain wrong. Even if she wasn't exactly a regular church attendee, she wouldn't use a church supper as an excuse to see a man. Would she?

It didn't matter. He probably was way too busy during the week to come to Wednesday-night dinner and devotionals anyway. That was mostly for the senior adult crowd that Grams hung with. Which made Goldie even more determined not to go as the poor still-single granddaughter of Ruth Rios. She'd get too many questions and innuendos from well-meaning but clueless senior citizens.

Ruth opened the door, the smell of vanilla lotion wafting into the room. She was dressed and ready, wearing a bright red Christmas sweater with gold metallic threads shooting through it. Leaning on her walker, she said, "It's my first time back at church since my surgery, honey. I'd really like it if you came with me."

Goldie pushed away from her laptop. "You can't go to church, Grams. You can't drive yourself yet. Doctor's orders."

"I'm not," Ruth corrected, her handbag already on her arm. "You're driving me. So you might as well stay and eat and hear Reverend Howe's devotional, too."

"But I'm not ready," Goldie replied, her gaze lingering on the big cup of coffee she'd just poured. "I'm in my sweats."

"All the more reason to hurry up and get dressed," Ruth proposed. "It's casual, so you don't have to fuss."

"But I thought Phyllis usually picked you up for church events anyway. Didn't she do that a lot before your surgery?"

Ruth's expression bordered on agitation. Placing her hands together over the bars on her walker, she explained, "Phyllis is way across town running errands and I'm not going to make her go out of her way when I have a perfectly good driver staying here in my home."

Goldie knew defeat when she saw it. And it shined brightly triumphant all over her grandmother's face. She also knew that Phyllis being across town didn't mean a whole lot, considering how small this town actually was. But when Grams got a notion in her mind, it didn't go away.

Goldie let out a sigh. "I'll be ready in ten minutes."

"Good." Grams shut the door with a soft victory swish.

Goldie stared down at her computer, wondering why she couldn't just tell her grandmother no sometimes. But she knew the answer to that. Grams had depended on Goldie for a long time now, since Angela wasn't in the picture as far as being a caring daughter-in-law. And Goldie depended on Grams to be her grandmother and mother, since Angela wasn't a caring mother, either. It was a mutual, unspoken rule around here. And even though Goldie had traveled a lot herself, she'd settled down to a pretty normal routine after she'd taken the job in Baton Rouge. Her work was just flexible enough to allow her travel time if she needed it and sometimes she did travel on assignment. It worked for her. And that was why she was here in Viola.

So she could be near Grammy, to help her.

And so Grammy could return the favor.

That was why Goldie was now rushing to throw on a green sweater and a black skirt and matching boots. Eyeing herself in the mirror, she decided there wasn't much she could do about the big bandage covering one half of her head, so she grabbed a wool hat with an embroidered blue and green flower woven into its seams, hoping that it would add some dash to her church-going ensemble.

"I'll get back to you later," she promised Shipwrecked.

After she figured out how to fix the clutter that seemed to be blocking her own nonexistent love life.

Rory watched as Goldie entered the church fellowship hall with her grandmother. Goldie held Ruth's arm, taking time to let her grandmother push her walker slowly up the aisle. They stopped to greet people, Ruth hugging and laughing while Goldie hung back as if she'd just walked into a dark forest. She actually looked afraid. But the cute hat made her look jaunty in spite of that lost expression on her face.

Goldie Rios obviously didn't like venturing into unknown territory. But the woman was supposed to be a world traveler and Rory knew that took courage and smarts. So why did she seem so out of place in Viola?

Or was she just out of place inside a church?

He kept watching her while his mother watched him. The boys were safely behind closed doors enjoying a tailor-made children's program and their own dinner, so for the next hour, he didn't have that responsibility. It was kind of nice to just watch a woman, to study her habits, to get to know her through her expressions and her body language.

Whoa! Rory reminded himself Goldie wasn't one of his wild animals, even if she did have that deer-in-the-headlights expression on her pretty face.

"Rory, it's rude to stare," his mother whispered in his ear.

He glanced at Frances, saw the disapproval in her eyes and wondered if he didn't have a new kind of war on his hands. His mother, usually so serene and even-tempered, seemed determined to thwart his attempts at flirting with a woman. Or at least with this particular woman. "Mom, I found her hurt and unconscious in my house last weekend. And she lost her necklace, probably at my house somewhere. It's natural that I'd want to make sure she is all right."

"She looks fit as a fiddle to me," Frances noted, her tone full of sarcasm. "And I'm sure she has a lot of jewelry, so quit worrying about that locket."

If they hadn't been in church, Rory might have retorted something back, but he wouldn't get into this with his mother in the Lord's house. He could understand her need to protect him, but he was a grown man.

"I'm a grown man," he said before he could grab his tongue.

"I happen to know that." Frances aimed her chin

toward Goldie. "And I'm pretty sure she's noticed, too."

He grinned at his mother. "I hope so."

Frances gave him a sharp-edged glare but didn't voice any hostile words. Thankfully, the preacher entered the building and quieted everyone so he could bless the meal of beef stew and biscuits provided by the Women's Prayer Group. That ended any further conversation regarding Goldie Rios.

But Rory did take his time looking at her when he buttered a biscuit or passed the dessert brownies. And when she glanced around after she'd settled her grandmother in a chair at the end of the long table across from Rory, her eyes locked with his and he smiled a greeting.

Goldie nodded then turned to face front and…never once looked back during the entire meal or Reverend Howe's interesting devotional.

Rory *was* here. Goldie kept thinking that as she ate her stew and chatted with Grammy's friends. He was here and even two brownies hadn't helped stifle her curiosity. He'd told her that he attended her grandmother's church and even though the thought of seeing him here had crossed her mind several times as she'd hurried to get ready, Goldie hadn't figured he'd actually show up on a Wednesday night. She folded her devotional sheet and put it in her purse, wondering if she should say hi to Rory. She'd kept her mind on the reverend's talk but the whole time she could almost feel Rory's eyes centered on the back of her head.

Or rather, on the back of her hat.

"Goldie, are you ready?"

She turned to find Grammy staring at her with a fixed expression. Everyone else was getting up to leave now that the closing prayer was over. "Oh, sorry. Yes, I'm ready."

"Did you have an extra prayer on your mind?" Grams asked sweetly. "Reverend Howe could pray with you."

"You could say that," Goldie replied, standing to help her grandmother into the aisle. Pushing the walker toward Ruth, she added, "But I'm good, Grams. I don't need to talk to the preacher."

"I'm so glad you came with me tonight, honey. You could use the Lord's centering in your life, you know."

Her grandmother might just have a point. The devotional had helped Goldie in a weird kind of way. Reverend Howe had talked about worrying, or rather, how to stop worrying—based on a passage in the book of Matthew. Goldie could use that advice, for sure. She did worry; she worried about keeping things in order. She worried about her job and never missing a deadline. She worried about being on time and trying to look and do her best. She worried that her best wasn't good enough. And she worried that this was it—this was as good as her life was going to get.

But why? What did worrying accomplish, except

more worrying? Turning some of that over to the Lord might just do the trick if she gave it a serious shot, at least. But right now, she was really worried about whether she should avoid Rory or say hello to him.

Then she remembered she had a legitimate question to ask him. She could ask about her locket—again—just in case. Which was good, because he was coming up behind her on the aisle. She caught sight of him when she turned to greet one of her grandmother's friends.

"Hi." Rory pulled Goldie to the side, smiling at her and hoping to wipe that look of unease off her face. "How are you?"

"I'm good," she said, brushing at her hat. "Grams kind of sprung this on me, so I didn't have much time to style my hair."

"And you're hiding the bandage, right?"

"You got me there. It's not a pretty sight."

"I like the hat."

She touched it again. "Thanks. It did keep my head warm."

She must be too warm; she had a nice flush going on.

"No more dizziness?"

She looked uncertain then shook her head. "No, not from the concussion, at least."

Her blush indicated maybe he could be the reason she was getting a little light-headed. And for some reason, that made him feel the same way. "Well, I just wanted to say hello. We're going home to finish homework."

"Oh, homework," she repeated, clutching her purse to her side. "I guess with two kids, you'd have a lot of that. Hey, did you happen to look for my locket again?"

He glanced down at the patterned carpet in the church hall. "Every time I've had a chance. I didn't find anything outside the house but we have a lot of leaves that need raking. And I did search again in the den and kitchen. Even took out the vacuum cleaner and hoped I'd hit on the necklace that way. Found a lot of lost toys and coins, but no necklaces. I'm sorry."

"Okay. I guess I've lost it for sure this time."

Surprised, Rory asked, "Have you misplaced it before?"

"No, not really. I have a spot for it back at home—right on top of my dresser. But here, in Grammy's spare bedroom, I just have a small travel case and I usually put it in there. I like things to be in their proper place."

She sure got all flustered when things weren't right where she expected them to be, or so it seemed from the few times he'd been around her. "Uh-huh."

Crestfallen, she lifted her chin in a brave front. "I've been known to toss it in there amid all the other jewelry I have with me, though. But it always turns up."

"Well, don't give up on it yet. It might be underneath the couch cushions and I just haven't touched on it yet."

She gave a shaky nod. "I owe you a new cushion, too."

"You do?"

"Yes. I'm pretty sure I left a bloodstain on your other one."

"I did put it in the laundry room. But it was already pretty messy from pizza and ice cream stains."

She smiled at that. "Well, Grammy's giving me the eye. This dinner was one of her first big outings, so I'm sure she's tired. I'd better get her home and all tucked in."

Rory could imagine Goldie tucking her grandmother into bed and making sure Ruth was comfortable and safe. That image made his heart soften into a pile of mush. He was about to tell her goodbye when he felt a hand on his arm. Rory's mother smiled at him. "The boys are getting restless."

"Oh, sorry, Mom. I'm coming." Rory looked back at Goldie. "Goldie Rios, this is my mother, Frances Branagan."

"Hello, Mrs. Branagan," Goldie greeted, reaching out a hand to his mother, her eyes bright with sincerity and curiosity.

Frances took her hand and smiled at her. "So this is the famous Goldie. How are you doing? No more head pain, I hope."

"I'm fine," Goldie reassured, grinning. "Just a few stitches and an ugly bandage."

To her credit, Frances was the very essence of politeness. "I'm glad you're all better. You gave Rory and the boys quite a scare."

A rush of little feet stopped the conversation. "Hey, it's her. The pretty lady who almost died on our couch!"

Rory winced as everyone around them turned to look after Tyler's loud announcement. "Tyler, use your inside voice," he cautioned.

"Too late for that," Frances pointed out, her tone firm but indulgent. "Tyler, it's time to go."

But Tyler was now clinging to Goldie's sweater. "You didn't die, did you?"

"No, I'm alive and well," Goldie said, her eyes wide with wonder and embarrassment. Then she leaned down. "And I do appreciate all your help."

Tyler grinned up at her. "All I did was stand there and get in the way."

That made her laugh. And caused something like a delicate snowflake to shimmy down inside Rory's soul.

Goldie looked up at Rory and Frances. "He is adorable, just like Grams said."

Frances let out an unladylike snort. "Yeah, right."

Sam walked up, his expression bordering on hostile. "Dad, I've got math to do."

Rory shot his oldest son a warning look. "Sam, don't be so rude. Can't you say hello to our friend Goldie?"

Sam stared at Goldie, but refused to acknowledge her. "Can we go now?"

Frances pulled at Sam's shirt collar. "Not until you show some manners, young man. Your father wants you to say hello."

"Hello!" Sam yelled an exaggerated holler, causing even more people to stop and stare.

Goldie's smile looked pasted on this time. She shifted her gaze from Sam to Rory then back to Sam. "Hi, Sam. It's good to see you again. And at least I'm not seeing two of you tonight."

Sam did a fake laugh. "Ha-ha. That's funny."

Rory felt the red all the way down to his toes. This was going from bad to worse. And he'd only stopped to greet Goldie at church. Imagine what his family might do if he did actually ask the woman out on a date.

He knew the answer to that. They'd all make him pay one way or another. Was he so wrong to want to get to know Goldie better?

Giving Goldie one last apologetic glance, he said, "I guess we'll see you later. I'll keep looking for your locket, I promise."

"Oh, okay then." She waved to him as Tyler and Sam dragged him down the steps. "Thanks."

Sam pulled away to turn and stare at Goldie. "We don't have her stupid necklace, Dad."

Rory pushed the boys into the car then closed the door on his mother's questioning expression.

Then he got in, took a deep breath and announced, "I guess I won't have to worry about ever dating a woman with you three around. Y'all embarrassed Goldie in there."

"I tried to be nice," Frances replied, her tone low and pensive.

"I just wanted to keep her," Tyler reminded them. "But y'all wouldn't let me."

"I hate her," Sam retorted, glaring at Rory in the rearview mirror. "And I'm sick of hearing about that dumb necklace she lost."

Frances gasped. "Sam, that is no way to talk."

Rory turned in his seat. "You and I are going to have a long discussion on manners when we get home, son. You know better than to talk like that to an adult. In fact, we don't talk to anyone in such a bad tone, ever."

Sam hung his head, his lips jutted out in a firm pout.

Frances gave him a hard stare then shrugged. "I'm sorry, Rory."

"Yeah, me, too."

Rory cranked the car and left the church parking lot. But he did notice Goldie in the glow of the outside church lights, watching as he drove away. And he could only imagine what she must be thinking.

Chapter Six

Two days later, Goldie was thinking of Rory Branagan. Again.

"I have to stop this," she whispered to herself as she fingered her hair. The gauze bandage was gone, but she did have a sore spot underneath the new part in her hair. And it was itching.

Just like her curious mind was itching with questions. Such as, why did she feel so drawn to this man? And why did one of his sons want to adopt her while the other one seemed to hate her? And what about his mother? Bad vibes there, no doubt. Was Frances Branagan being overly protective or did she see something in Goldie that didn't impress her enough to want Goldie to get to know her son?

Can't blame her, Goldie thought as she wrapped up the ending paragraph of her blog. She'd already sent her weekly column, and yes, she'd answered Shipwrecked's question with authority and aplomb, the point being if your home is cluttered then you probably have underlying emotional clutter to clear out, too.

But what if you ran screaming from clutter and messy situations? Goldie wondered. She'd been doing that for most of her life. And she knew, deep in her soul, that all the moving around and traveling had only worsened her compulsive nature. And now, she'd made a career out of keeping clutter at bay.

When are you going to delve into your own overpacked mess of emotions? The voice in her head played that loop over and over again while Goldie just kept pushing it away.

She looked at the tidy little room that had become her haven over the last few weeks, taking in the blue-and-brown-striped curtains and deep brown bedspread with the blue flower sprigs she'd bought at the superstore on the highway. Her gaze moved over the matching canvas baskets and containers she'd placed on an old bookshelf next to the many research books she had brought with her. The dainty old desk she'd found in the shed out back had been restored to a sky blue. Her laptop and a white pencil holder sat pristinely on the desk, her papers stacked and sorted and arranged just so by her open spiral-bound day calendar. A brown vase of freshly cut mums left over from Grammy's fall garden brightened the room. And the one picture on the wall reflected a rocking chair set against a white porch, the blues of the flowers along the brown steps in the picture perfectly matching the color scheme of this room. She'd done that, made this room her home for now. Until it was time to move on.

She'd come here after Grammy's surgery and reorganized almost the whole house in between trips to the hospital and then later chauffeuring Grams to the rehab unit, working at her laptop in the lobby while Grams went through therapy. Grams had come home to a better-organized house, her shock evident even when she'd thanked Goldie for making everything so convenient for her.

And Goldie had gotten two columns and three blog posts out of the whole makeover, passing on tips and suggestions to her readers with delight. Not bad. Not bad at all.

But there was still that tangled mess inside her mind that needed to be sorted. And thinking about Rory only made the tangle even crazier—and harder to unravel.

Her laptop dinged with a new e-mail. Goldie glanced at it then opened the message.

Dear Goldie:

Thanks for the advice you gave to "Shipwrecked in Serepta." I feel the same way sometimes. I'm not a very neat person but I'd like to have more control in my life. I've tried sorting through magazines and catalogs with plans to

> just toss them, but they always seem to pile up around me again. Sometimes I order things I don't even need or want. How can I stay on top of all the trash that seems to accumulate in my house and stop buying things I don't really need?
>
> —Buried in Bossier City

Goldie stared down at the words on her screen. She'd have to carefully consider this, do some research with the experts and get back to Buried. Because this was about more than just catalogs and magazines and all the pretty enticements such things offered. This was about having an orderly life and making sure all the stacks and stacks of junk didn't bury the real issues. Whatever the real issues might be.

She saved the message then grabbed her cell phone and stood to go outside. Maybe a short walk would get rid of this restlessness. Passing where Grams sat knitting as she watched the evening news, Goldie tossed a wrap over her shoulders and called out, "I'll be in the backyard getting some fresh air if you need me, Grammy. I have my phone so you can page me."

Grammy shifted then held up her own phone. "Got mine right here handy." Giving Goldie a glance, she added, "It's a Friday night. Shouldn't you be out with people your own age?"

Goldie laughed out loud. "In case you haven't noticed, there aren't a whole lot of people my age living in Viola."

Grams chuckled. "What about your friend Carla from Baton Rouge? She could drive up and spend the weekend here with us."

"Yeah, I'm sure Carla will jump right on that idea." Then because Grams looked confused, she said, "It's okay. I'm fine. We'll watch a movie after supper, okay?"

"If I can stay awake that long," Ruth replied.

Goldie went out the back door, her boots hitting against dry leaves and crunchy winter grass. It was just hitting that cold time of evening when the sun officially became a golden glow behind the horizon and dusk blanketed the air with a crisp intensity. That time between work and coming home, she thought. She tugged the long wool wrap around her neck. Maybe she should have grabbed a jacket, but she'd only be out here a few minutes.

Then she heard a sound coming from the concrete canal just beyond her grandmother's property line. Such canals and aqueducts were common in flood-prone, flat Louisiana. But that sound wasn't so common. It came again, a yelp of pain. Deciding there must be a wounded animal down there, Goldie pushed through the trees and shrubs and glanced across the chain-link fence. Then she saw a movement in the bramble where a puddle of old mud, tree limbs and leaves had pooled near one of the drains.

Another yelp caused her to gasp. A black and white

puppy was down there and from the looks of things, the poor baby had become trapped in some washed-up rope and old vines. "Hold on, little fellow."

Goldie didn't hesitate. She immediately ran to the crooked chain-link gate and opened it, determined to make her way down the side of the slippery canal so she could untangle the shivering animal below. But the concrete ditch was steep and still moist from the storm. She held on to an old vine, hoping to use it for leverage so she could shimmy down the side of the concrete embankment.

"Hold on, little puppy. I'm coming."

The vine broke, sending Goldie right into the pile of tangled vines and wet, muddy leaves. With a whoosh, she hit bottom hard, landing right next to the trapped puppy. The dog started yelping, excitement and fear causing the scared animal to step back. But his little paw was all caught up in the mess.

"Hold on, baby," Goldie cooed after she'd caught her breath. "Let me see if I broke anything."

She sat there, the wetness seeping into her jeans causing her to shiver and groan. "This doesn't feel so good." She would be bruised but she was probably all right. At least she hadn't hit her head again. Reaching across to the shaking little dog, Goldie lowered her voice. "It's okay, fellow. I promise. I'll get us out of here somehow."

But when she looked back up at the solid wall of aged concrete, she wondered at her own good sense.

Why hadn't she thought to bring a rope or a ladder at least?

"I guess we're in trouble," she confessed to the hyper dog. Trying anew to gain the animal's trust, she held her hand out, palm down, so he could sniff her knuckles.

The trembling little dog lifted his nostrils from his spot but didn't try to come any closer to Goldie. "I assure you I'm on your side," she said, looking around to see what she could do.

Dusk was setting in right on time. Cold air penetrated her wet clothes. Her lightweight sweater and wrap didn't help much. Her clothes were now sagging with mud. She could probably grab a vine or a low branch from one of the cypress trees but she was afraid that wouldn't hold her weight.

"Any suggestions?" she asked the anxious puppy.

He growled and yelped.

"I see. You're no help."

Goldie grabbed her cell phone out of her pocket. She'd have to call Grams to send help. And she had a feeling she knew exactly who Grams could call.

The nuisance hunter.

Rory had just finished washing the dinner plates when the phone rang. Glancing at the clock, he let out a sigh. And hoped he wouldn't be called out tonight. He'd been looking forward to a quiet night with the boys.

"Hello," he answered, bracing himself.

"Rory, it's Ruth Rios. I need your help."

Rory smiled in spite of his dread. "Not another armadillo, Miss Ruth?"

"No, not this time. It's Goldie. She's somehow gotten herself stuck in the drainage canal behind my house. She was trying to get to a little puppy and now they're both stuck. She's okay but she can't get back up the wall. Something about carrying the dog and too much mud and everything being slippery. I can't do anything to help her and she can't stay out there all night."

"I'll be right there," Rory said. He hung up the phone then turned to the boys. "C'mon, you two. We've got a mission."

"You're taking us with you?" Tyler asked, his big eyes going wide.

"Yep. Your grandmother is out with her church group tonight. And this should be an easy job. Y'all might get to help."

Sam didn't look so sure. "I have homework."

"Bring it with you. You can stay inside with Miss Ruth and finish up while I help Goldie."

Hostility oozed from Sam's pores. "We're going to that woman's house?"

"Yes, Sam, we are. Now don't argue with me. Just get your coat, your books and lesson plans and let's go. It's cold out there and Goldie is stuck in a ditch with a puppy."

"A puppy?" Tyler grabbed his down jacket. "You said *we* might get a puppy, remember?"

"I remember," Rory replied. He'd held off getting a pet for the boys because they were rarely home during the weekdays. And he wasn't so sure his sons were ready for that kind of responsibility. Maybe taking them on this rescue mission wasn't such a hot idea. "Let's just go help Goldie and Miss Ruth and we'll talk about that later."

"Maybe we can have *this* puppy," Tyler suggested, his tone relentless in its enthusiasm. "I'd like that."

Rory pinched his nose with his fingers. "Get in the truck, son."

The boys hopped into his big truck, one scowling and one smiling. It was gonna be another long night.

Goldie heard the roar of a truck's engine. Looking over at the dog she'd dubbed Spike because he reminded her of the Peanuts cartoon character that was Snoopy's cousin, she grinned. "Cavalry's here, Spike. We'll be inside by the fire in about five minutes, tops."

Spike had inched closer but he still shivered with resistance. But his yelps had turned into whimpers now.

"I know you're cold and scared," Goldie whispered, her hand reaching out to the dog, "but I'm here with you and Rory is a highly trained expert. He'll get us out of this, I promise." She stared up at the evening star over her head. "And so will God. God loves all creatures, you know. Even scruffy little dogs."

Spike whimpered then yelped with a more positive enthusiasm this time.

"Good. You understand. I like that in a dog."

"Well, aren't you two cozy down there."

Goldie turned to find Rory grinning at her.

And what a grin. His expression held amusement and concern all in one good-looking package. Or maybe what was left of the muted early-evening light was playing tricks on her. "Hey there. 'Bout time you got here."

Rory shook his head. "Why is it that I always find you in a dire situation?"

"Just call it the *Perils of Pauline,*" Goldie said, shrugging. "I could have found a way back up but I didn't want to leave Spike down here by himself."

"Of course not." Rory motioned behind him. "Tyler, stay right there. We might need you to help with…uh…Spike when we bring these two up."

Tyler peeked over the fence. "Hey, Miss Goldie. You found a puppy?"

Goldie nodded. "Sure did. And we've gotten pretty close over the last half hour. I think he's hungry and cold. And so am I."

Rory opened the gate then brought Grammy's ladder through. "Goldie, can you walk? I mean, you didn't damage anything, did you?"

"Nothing but my pride. That wet concrete doesn't have a lot of traction."

He looked around. "I can see that. I'm gonna unfold the ladder and hold it for you to come up, okay?"

"Okay, but what about Spike?"

"Will he come to you?"

"He might. He's still a little skittish, though. And I have to get him untangled, if he'll let me."

Rory turned to Tyler. "Son, run in the house and ask Miss Ruth for a piece of cheese. Tell Sam to get it for her."

"Okay." Tyler took off.

Rory faced Goldie. "I could come down there myself and try to free him."

"No, don't do that," Goldie argued. "He's just now gotten used to me. You'd probably scare him all over again. Maybe the food will help. If not, then you can give it a try."

"Okay, 'cause as much as I'm enjoying this lovely scene, I promised your grandmother I wouldn't leave you in this ditch."

Goldie smiled, happy for the company even if she was frozen solid. "So, are most of your Friday nights this exciting, Rory?"

"Not before you came along," he replied, that grin still intact. "You know, you're becoming more of a nuisance than any animals I've ever had to hunt."

"Sorry," she mumbled, his teasing words stinging her with a bite that beat the cold. "I didn't want Grams to call you, but she insisted you were the best man for the job."

He laughed at that. "I can't say I've ever had to rescue a human being before, that is—"

"I know, before I hit town. I'll try to be more careful after this."

He slanted his head. "If you didn't scare me so much with your mishaps, I'd tell you to keep it up. At least it's an excuse to see a pretty lady now and then, bleeding head and wet mud and yelping dogs aside."

"Very funny."

But those words hadn't stung at all. No, his *flirting* words poured over Goldie, warming her to the core in spite of his intentional references to her accident-prone existence. But the man did have a point. She always seemed to be in some sort of predicament in spite of touting herself as organized and completely together.

Then Tyler came running with the hunk of cheese. "I had to get it myself. Sam wouldn't help. But Miss Ruth told me right where to find it in the refrigerator."

The warmth left Goldie's soul. Sam didn't like her. And that could be a big problem since she didn't have a clue about handling a little boy. She didn't even have such a great track record with the big boys, either. So why was she even bothering with the idea of getting to know Rory better?

She stood and held out a hand to catch the cheese Rory tossed down. Then she turned to Spike, enticing him with the food. "Okay, fellow, you have to help me out here." She leaned close and whispered, "'Cause I think I could really fall for this one and I shouldn't do that for oh, so many reasons."

Spike barked at her then tugged to be free from his constraints. Seeing that as a good sign, Goldie carefully scooted toward the little dog, broke the cheese into tiny pieces and held out her hand again.

Spike strained toward her and licked her knuckles then after sniffing, ate the cheese from her hand. When he was finished, Goldie carefully lifted the squirming animal up and worked to free his paw from the twisted vines and coarse old rope that had snared him. Spike fidgeted and yelped a bit, but he looked up at Goldie with trusting eyes until she had him free.

"He's fallen for you," Rory said, his tone muted and low as it echoed out on the night air.

When Goldie turned around to stare up at him, she thought she saw something there in his glistening eyes.

Something that excited her even while it confused her.

"I know how you feel," she said to Spike. Then she scooped up the little dog in her arms and dragged her aching, wet self toward the ladder.

And took the hand of the man waiting there for her at the top.

"Good to see you again, Goldilocks," Rory teased as he lifted her onto the grass.

Goldie swallowed the lump in her throat. "Thanks for coming, Rory. Thanks again for helping me."

Rory tugged her wet wrap away then took off his own down jacket and wrapped it around Goldie and Spike.

"Let's get y'all inside to the fire."

Goldie looked down at Spike again, the warmth of Rory's jacket cocooning them like a security blanket.

"We're safe now, little fellow."

And she knew that she was safe, even if this man could be a big danger to her tattered emotions.

Chapter Seven

"Rory, that's a nice fire."

Rory put another log on then turned to smile at Ruth. The tiny lights on the Christmas tree by the window twinkled almost as much as her eyes. "I've had lots of practice." He sat down on the couch beside Tyler. "How's that hot chocolate, son?"

"Good," Tyler said. "Almost as good as Mee-Maw's."

Ruth laughed at that. "Grandmas always make the best." She glanced over to the tiny dining table where Sam sat reading a book, his brow wrinkled with a scowl. "Sam, would you like some more hot chocolate?"

Sam eyed Rory, saw the warning look Rory shot him then said, "No, ma'am. Thank you."

Goldie came into the living room, wearing clean clothes and carrying Spike in her arms. "I have a new shadow," she proclaimed, smiling down at the now-clean puppy. "I managed to wipe him down with a wet rag at least. Think I got most of the mud and leaves out of his fur."

Tyler rushed over. "Can I pet him, Miss Goldie?"

"Sure," Goldie responded. She sank down on a floral ottoman by the fire. "Just be careful. He's still kind of scared."

"I wonder if he got lost," Tyler said, carefully rubbing Spike's thick hair. "Or maybe somebody left him."

"I hope not," Ruth said. "It's not nice to leave a helpless little animal out in the cold on a night such as this."

"What kind of dog is he, Dad?" Tyler asked, still petting Spike. The dog settled into Goldie's lap and held his nose up to Tyler, obviously deciding he had yet another new friend.

Rory grinned. "I'd say he's a Sooner, son."

"What kind of dog is that?" Tyler asked.

"He'd sooner be one breed as another," Rory replied, winking at Goldie.

She laughed then held Spike up in the air. "You hear that, boy? I think you've been insulted."

"He doesn't care," Ruth stated. "He's safe and warm now and that's all that matters."

"Are you gonna keep him?" Tyler inquired of Goldie.

She looked over at Rory. "I'd like to, but I won't be able to take him back to Baton Rouge with me. My apartment doesn't allow pets."

"Then you oughta just stay here with Miss Ruth," Tyler claimed in a reasonable tone.

Rory saw Goldie's reaction to that. She got all flustered and fidgety. Which meant she wasn't planning on sticking around any longer than necessary.

"Tyler, Miss Goldie lives in the city and she's a very busy woman. She doesn't have time to keep a dog."

Goldie lifted her eyebrows in protest. "I didn't say that. I just said my lease agreement clearly states no pets."

"You could move," Tyler said, intent on helping out with this situation. "Or you could just give Spike to me. I'd take good care of him. Sam could help, right, Sam?"

"Yeah, whatever," Sam said, his tone full of disdain.

Rory watched Goldie's reaction to his eldest son's rudeness, wishing he could figure out what Sam's problem was. But he knew the boy had struggled since he'd lost his mother and no amount of talking to the church counselor or asking God for mercies had seemed to help.

Maybe adopting a dog would. "Sam, would you be willing to help take care of Spike if we took him?"

Sam slapped his book closed, but his eyes did grow wide with interest. "I don't care. Maybe."

"I care," Tyler said, jumping up to clap his hands. "Can we take him home, Daddy?"

Rory looked from Sam's frowning face to Tyler's hopeful one. "Not tonight, boys. We're not prepared and it's too late to get supplies tonight."

Of course, he could rustle up a doggie bed and some food easily enough but he wasn't ready to make a commitment until he figured out what to do about Sam's surly response. He wanted to teach his sons responsibility but first he'd have to see if Sam was willing to go the distance and help Tyler with the dog.

Goldie stood up, holding Spike close. "I have an idea. How about I keep him here with me and Grams until it's time for me to go back home after Christmas? That way, we can enjoy him and make him feel secure. And in the meantime, you can buy whatever you need to set up a home for him and maybe your daddy can go over some rules with you on how to care for an animal. How does that sound?"

Tyler looked confused at first then turned to Rory. "Dad, would that be okay?"

Rory shot Goldie an appreciative nod. "That just might work. But first, we have to convince your brother that he'd help you take care of Spike. Sam, you hear that?"

Sam glared at the little dog. "I don't care, I told you already. It's just a dumb animal." He went back to pretending to read but Rory noticed he glanced at the puppy a couple of times.

Ruth raised up in her chair. "Sounds as if Sam doesn't like dogs. I've never known a boy not to want a puppy." She shrugged, acting indifferent to Sam's attitude. "Oh, well. I guess if this plan isn't approved by all the Branagan men, then I might wind up with

Spike as my only companion once Goldie goes back to Baton Rouge. And me old and hardly able to walk. I'd have to get a sitter for the little fellow every time I go to therapy. And I can't even lift the poor animal. I'd worry constantly that he'd get loose and run away again. On the other hand, I could certainly babysit Spike for whoever else he winds up with. That would be easier on me—and Spike, too, I imagine." She let out a long, dramatic sigh. "I guess after Goldie leaves, I'll have to put an ad in the paper to find him a suitable home. If only—"

"I didn't say no," Sam countered, his tone quieter now. He rubbed a hand across his nose. "I'd have to think about it some more and find out what needs to be done, is all."

Ruth clapped her hands together in glee. "That sounds like a logical process. Rory, you never told me how smart Sam is. He's taking his time so as not to rush into this lightly and I think that's very wise. Taking care of someone else is hard work, as we adults well know."

Rory wanted to kiss Miss Ruth. Instead, he glanced over at Goldie. "So you're gonna keep Spike for now?"

"Yes, I am," she agreed, nuzzling the dog. "He's really a sweet puppy." Then she looked at Sam. "But when it's time for me to leave, I hope y'all can take him. And I hope you'll bring him back to visit Grams now and then. That would make me feel better."

Sam eyed Rory, his scowl gone for now. But the frustration and disappointment showing on his face was almost worse than any scowl. "What if he belongs to someone else, Dad? Then we'd have to give him back."

Rory's heart hurt for his son. Maybe Sam was afraid to love again. Rory sure knew that feeling.

Ruth let out a gasp before Rory could respond. "See how smart he is. Sam's right. Maybe we should ask around before we go making plans for our new friend."

"I'll do that," Goldie said. "I'll put out flyers around the neighborhood and ask some of the neighbors if they're missing a pet. Good thinking, Sam."

Sam lowered his head again. "Can we go now, Dad?"

"Yes," Rory said, getting up. "It is a school night. Did you get all your lessons done?"

Sam nodded. "Miss Ruth helped me with some of the spelling."

"Did you thank her?"

Ruth bobbed her head. "He certainly did. We had a nice visit, too. Although I couldn't figure why he'd want to sit here with an old lady while y'all were out there, rescuing Spike."

Sam lifted his gaze toward Goldie then lowered his head. "I just wanted to get my homework done."

Rory motioned for the boys. "C'mon, you two. Let's get going." He waited until they'd both located their jackets. "Tell Miss Ruth thanks for the hot chocolate then head to the truck."

"Thanks," they spoke in unison.

After the boys gathered their things, Ruth pulled herself up and grabbed on to her walker, giving both of them a one-armed hug. "I think I'm going to bed. Good night all."

Rory glanced from her slowly departing form to Goldie and the dog. "Boys, go ahead now. I'll be there in just a minute."

Sam gave him a skeptical look. "Dad—"

"Go, Sam. Now."

Sam and Tyler went up the hall and out the front door.

"I'm sorry about Sam's attitude," Rory told Goldie.

She nodded. "I understand. He's a little boy and he misses his mother. He thinks I'm a threat to that—to all of you. I don't have to be a psychologist to see that."

"I miss her, too," Rory replied. "Tyler's still too young to grasp what happened, but Sam—he was older and he saw what it did to me. I guess some of that rubbed off on him."

Goldie handed him Spike. Taking the dog, Rory rubbed the soft fur on the animal's back and was rewarded with a lick on the face. "Maybe a dog would help."

She stared over at Spike. "He is adorable." Then she addressed Rory. "Grams told me what happened with your wife. A robbery, Rory, such a senseless crime. I can't imagine what you must have gone through."

Rory didn't like to talk about this, but he felt Goldie needed to understand. "She just went for some milk and eggs. She was baking and I had promised I'd get the stuff on the way home. But I had an emergency and so she went herself. The boys were at a Scout meeting. I was gonna pick them up then swing by the grocery store. Instead, she went to a convenience store near our house to save time. And she got shot, right there in the store. Her and the store clerk. The clerk survived."

He couldn't look at Goldie, so he held tightly to the little dog and stared down into Spike's dark, expectant eyes. "Maybe a dog *would* help."

He heard Goldie's sharp intake of breath then looked up at her, seeing the anguish on her face. "Goldie, I—"

"You don't owe me any explanations, Rory." She took the dog back. "Thanks for saving Spike and me."

Rory didn't know what else to say. They didn't have much of a chance, him and Goldie. He knew it and she knew it. There was just so much between them. So much left unsaid. Grief and distance and circumstances and life. But he did know that since he'd met Goldie Rios, something inside him had changed. He stared at the fidgety little dog then glanced at Goldie. "Some things are worth saving, no matter the cost."

Spike pressed his nose against Goldie's sweater. Rory looked at her, his gaze holding hers. She didn't speak. She just stood there. Rory had the sudden urge to kiss her. He held his fists to his sides, telling himself that kissing her would only make things worse. "I guess I'd better go before the boys hijack my truck and run it into the bayou."

She smiled at that. Then she turned serious again. "Rory, it's okay. Really. I understand."

Rory clinched his fists again. "No, it's not okay. I should be able to ask you out on a proper date. But—"

"But you have two little boys and you have responsibilities and…you're still grieving." She held Spike close. "And I'll be going back to Baton Rouge soon anyway."

"It's only an hour's drive."

"But we're still a long way from that."

He stepped close then. "But while you're here…"

"While I'm here, let's just leave things the way they are, for everyone's sake, okay?"

"Could you just tell me this, then? What if…say things were okay and I did ask you out on a date? Would you go, I mean, if we didn't have all these complications holding us back?"

She glanced down at Spike then back up and into his eyes. "If things were different, yes, I'd go out with you. But I remembered what happened the day of my wreck. I'd just broken up with a man who bought a puppy for another woman the same day he was supposed to have a romantic dinner with me. That kind of scars a girl, if you know what I mean."

He nodded. "Yeah, I get that." Then he pointed to Spike. "But look at you now. You have your own puppy."

"Only I had to get him the hard way."

"Or maybe God sent him just in time. You saved this little dog, Goldie. You think I'm the one doing all the rescuing around here, but I think you've got that all backward. You're pretty good at rescues yourself."

"No, I'm pretty good at bluffing my way through life."

"So you're telling me you're just a big joke? A sham?"

"Something like that."

He finally gave in and leaned close. "You are so wrong on that account, Goldilocks. I've felt more alive since you've come in my life than I have for months now. And that's a sure sign that I need to focus on my boys a little more, that I need to feel alive for them. So I thank you for making me see that."

"Whatever I can do to help."

He saw the disappointment in her eyes but he heard the message in her words. He did need to focus on his boys. And that was that.

"Take care of Spike."

"I will," she said, her tone full of resignation. "And I'll bring him to the boys whenever it's time for me to leave, I promise."

Rory nodded then turned toward the door. He'd

hold her to that promise, if only because it would give him one more chance to see her again before she walked out of his life forever.

Goldie lay curled in bed, Spike snuggled on an old blanket right beside her. Amazing how a lost little animal could bring out all her maternal instincts. But it was the scowl of a lost little boy that was keeping her awake tonight. That and the hurt expression in his daddy's eyes whenever Rory looked at her.

He's drawn to me, she thought, her hand stroking Spike's fur. And I feel something. She'd never felt so much so quickly with the men she'd thought she cared about.

Lord, what's happening to me?

She'd come here to help her grandmother, to do the right thing in her wayward mother's absence. She'd come here for a temporary time, determined to keep up with her obligations and to do her job, determined to keep the fragile order in her life, the order that kept her sane, content and committed. But what kind of order did she really have? She had traveled when she only wanted to settle down. She had organized and arranged when in her mind, her life was in disarray and disrepair. She missed her father, longed for her mother, loved her grandmother. Believed in God even when she didn't dare darken the doors of church unless forced to do so. She felt alone, so alone at times that the intensity of it pierced her very soul.

"What's happening?" she asked in her prayers. Was she so busy trying to make things perfect that she'd missed making things right?

Spike made a cute little snoring noise. The dog knew he was safe now, and he felt secure in his slumbers. Someone had heard his pleas, had listened to his distress. Goldie longed for that kind of security.

Some things are worth saving.

Rory's words came back to her, there in the silence of a winter night. And she wondered if he was sending out his own plea for help.

Do I try to save him, Lord? Or do I just walk away before I get hurt again?

Goldie didn't have any answers for that. But she'd sure been willing to fight for this lost little animal. Wasn't Rory worth fighting for, too? Weren't Rory and his sons worth saving, same as little Spike?

"Uh-oh." Goldie sat up, causing Spike to do the same. Her whole system was now on high alert. Spike sensed her confusion. He nuzzled his way onto her lap then tried to lick her face.

Her instincts told her that she needed to fix this situation, to make it right. But her heart told her that she couldn't make something perfect out of something that was broken, maybe beyond repair. How did she find the perfect solution for a grieving man and his two confused little boys? Grams always said to pray, just pray.

And so Goldie did. For a long time. She poured out

her thoughts to God and asked His guidance. She waited for the peace of an unburdened heart, the peace that Grams seemed to possess even in the worst of circumstances. Finally, drained and tired, she grabbed at the covers then burrowed deep underneath the blankets, Spike yelping at her to let him in. Goldie brought the little dog close beside her again and watched as he settled down, but it was a long time before *she* finally went to sleep.

Chapter Eight

"I was beginning to think I'd never see you again."

Carla McCoy walked around Goldie's bedroom in her grandmother's house, picking up knickknacks as she admired the new decorating scheme. Spike followed Goldie's best friend, sniffing at her loafers each time she stopped, his little paws skidding on the hardwood floor.

"I've been right here," Goldie replied from her spot on the bed. She patted the comforter and laughed as Spike took a running jump toward her. "Except for that fateful night I went to the mall to do some shopping and, oh yeah, caught my boyfriend with another woman."

"You need to get out more," Carla said, her short red shag falling around her ears. "You sound kind of bitter."

"I'm not bitter about having to be here with

Grams," Goldie replied. "But yes, I'm a tad frustrated about my ex-boyfriends."

Carla plopped down beside her. "So that's why you've been as quiet as a church mouse for the last week or so. You lying low, hoping to hide out here in little Viola forever just because of some man who didn't know a good thing when he saw it?"

"Just through the holidays," Goldie retorted. "I'm not hiding out but I am lying low. That's been the plan since Grammy had her surgery, anyway. I'm staying here until Angela gets back from her grand tour of Europe. And then I'm sure my mother will be ever so eager to check up on Grams now and then."

"You're bitter about your mother, too, aren't you?"

Goldie thought about that for a minute. "I'm not mad that she traipsed off to Europe even after Grams fell and broke her hip, no, because that's how Angela deals with things—she runs away. And I don't mind one bit hanging out with Grams. I've been doing that most of my life and I love it."

Carla tilted her head, her golden bell earrings making a tinkling sound. "But?"

"My daddy loved Grams. I mean, she was his mother and all that. But my mother and Grams? Not so good. Friction every time they get together—like sandpaper hitting rough rocks or something. So technically, it wouldn't have been a good mix—my mother here with her mother-in-law for weeks on end. Mama thinks Grams is too straitlaced and churchy, and Grams thinks Mama is too loose and flighty, if you know what I mean?"

Carla let out a hoot of laughter. "I don't know about your mother, but your Grammy is one of the coolest people I've ever met, Goldie. How could anyone not love Miss Ruth?"

"My mama loves Grams," Goldie countered. "She just can't be in the same room with her for more than five minutes. I mean, Grams is settled and sure of things while my mother is scatterbrained and not very capable of making a coherent decision. So that's why I have to run interference."

"But you can't run interference forever."

Goldie shrugged. "I can and I will. It's what family is all about. I've always been the peacemaker, the one who kept my mother organized and on track and the one who stuck by Grammy because she was so organized and on track. I took over where my dad left off, I reckon."

"You've done a good job, considering Miss Ruth doesn't have anyone else to help her out." Carla twirled her hair with a finger. "I know she has lots of church friends and that's good, but family is important. Family is just better."

"And that's why I'm here," Goldie said, her thoughts drifting to Rory and his duty to his family. "I'm blessed that my job allows me to work from home a lot and that my boss at the paper was willing to permit this extended long-distance work relationship, so I was the logical choice."

"Not a lot of granddaughters would do that, you know," Carla replied, getting up to roam around again. Spike took that as a sign he needed to do the same.

Carla scooped the little dog into her arms. "You are so cute," she told Spike. "And much more understanding and interesting than most men, I must admit." She leaned close to whisper to Spike, "I'm so glad my friend here has you to talk to while she's…uh…lying low."

Goldie grinned. "I didn't have much choice since no one responded to my flyers or queries. I couldn't abandon the poor little fellow. And Grams loves him, too."

Carla stroked Spike's back. "You seem to like it here."

Goldie looked at her friend, making a face. "I think I needed this time away from Baton Rouge. It's been good for me, taking things easy over the last few weeks." She shrugged. "And that's probably part of the reason Loser Number Five was buying a puppy for another woman in the mall in the first place. I neglected him and his fragile ego."

"Did he bother to come here and see you, before you spotted him with her?" Carla asked.

"He came a few times and we'd go out to dinner, but I knew something was up," Goldie admitted. "We never were a sure thing from the beginning, but I held out hope."

"Don't we all," Carla said, putting Spike on the bed

then turning to unpack her weekend bag. Spike stood on his hind legs and nosed into the bag, but she pushed him away.

"Is that why you decided to come and visit?" Goldie questioned, glad to see her friend but still wondering what Carla was doing here when she preferred the nightlife in Baton Rouge over a quiet weekend in the country.

"I'll tell you all the latest tonight, after we do our nails, eat popcorn and watch sappy movies," Carla promised. "But I do have some good news. I think I've actually found a man I can settle down with."

Goldie got up and touched a hand to her friend's sweater sleeve. "Oh, then I have to hear the details on that."

"All in good time," Carla said. "I just need some solid advice. I'm kind of scared I might make a mess of things."

"That would be my department," Goldie quipped.

"We'll talk later," Carla repeated. "I promise."

"Okay, whenever you're ready to talk. In the meantime, I'm glad you called and I'm glad you came. Want to go get Mexican for dinner?"

"Can you leave Grams?"

"I can now, yes. She has her cell and I have mine, just in case. And she has one of those emergency necklaces. She wears that all the time."

"Mexican it is, then," Carla agreed. "Besides, the restaurant isn't that far away, is it?"

"Nothing in this town is that far away," Goldie said through a grin. But her grin faded when she thought about Rory's house just a few miles down the road. Best not to remember the big Christmas tree and the pretty kitchen. Or the fact that Rory was usually in that kitchen every night, trying to be a good father to his boys.

Carla grabbed her purse. "I'll just freshen up and then I'll be ready. And, Goldie, when we get to the restaurant, I want *you* to tell me all about this nuisance hunter you keep mentioning in your calls and e-mails. That can't wait until later and lights out. I have to know all of it ASAP."

Goldie shook her head. "I was hoping you wouldn't ask about that."

Carla laughed as she headed toward the bathroom. "No such luck, girl. There's something in your voice whenever you mention this new man in your life."

Goldie heard the bathroom door shut then turned to stare at her reflection in the dresser mirror. "Something's there, all right." She just wasn't sure what that something was.

She thought about all the reasons she shouldn't get involved with Rory Branagan—his grief, his sullen older son, his disapproving but well-meaning mother, Goldie's own aversion to yet another failed relationship, her job in the city, her need to stay organized and in control.

Not a whole lot going for them.

If you didn't count the way just seeing the man made her go all soft and gooey inside. Or the fact that he'd rescued her twice now and always made her feel safe and secure by smiling at her.

She looked down at Spike. "Or you, little bit. I can't forget that you are the tie that is binding Rory and me together right now."

Because she would soon be handing off Spike to Rory, for safekeeping. Her heart might also go with the little dog when that handoff took place.

And then she'd go back to the real world and her loneliness again.

The loneliness had never bothered him this much.

Rory stared out at the looming night, wondering what to do with himself. His sister had brought her kids from Dallas to visit with his mother and his boys. Becky had offered to give both Rory and Frances a night off by taking her two girls and his boys out for pizza and a movie. Frances was doing her last-minute Christmas shopping.

Which left Rory alone on a Friday night.

He could wrap presents or watch a game on the sports channel. Or he could just stand here staring out the window, wondering what Goldie was doing tonight. But that wouldn't do and thinking about Goldie made him much lonelier.

He went to the Christmas tree, smiling at the collection of ornaments they'd gathered over the years.

Two "Baby's First Christmas" balls with the dates of his sons' births printed on them in gold make him remember when his children had come into the world. He looked over the tree, searching for the "First Christmas Together" ornament his mother had given to him and Rachel after they'd gotten married. It was white porcelain and had two little bears dressed in snow clothes kissing. Rachel had loved that ornament. Then he noticed the picture ornaments showing his boys at various ages. Rory touched a hand to each one, his memories as warm and vibrant as the fire that roared in the fireplace. Why were the holidays so hard?

He closed his eyes to lift up a prayer for peace and control. He had to be strong for his children, had to be understanding whenever Sam acted out or Tyler cried in the night for his mother. The horror of Rachel's death still haunted Rory, filling him with guilt. Life was so precious. It could all change in one minute. He thought about the night he'd found Goldie right here in this room.

What if she'd died that night?

He would never have known her pretty smile or her dry wit. He wouldn't have been able to watch her golden curls rustling like twirling silk around her face. He would have never seen her cuddling Spike, the sight of that simple sign of affection causing his worn, tired heart to swell and pump a little faster. He would never have known Goldie.

"What do I do now, Lord?" he asked out loud. "Should I listen to my heart, or keep cool and just let her go?"

Rory didn't have the answers to those questions and tonight, he didn't want to think about next year and Goldie going back to Baton Rouge. Besides, Baton Rouge wasn't that far away and he was sure Goldie would come and visit Ruth more often now. Wouldn't she?

He'd just have to take things slowly and leave it all in God's hands. What else could he do?

You could be a little more aggressive, a little more proactive, he told himself. You could go after Goldie.

He could, but he wouldn't.

Rory stared up at the tree again, the faces of his boys smiling, gap-toothed and innocent, back at him.

No, he wouldn't pursue Goldie. He had to think of his children. But what if having Goldie in their lives could make a positive difference for his boys?

Rory had never thought of that, considering how surly Sam had been around Goldie. But Tyler wanted to keep Goldie in their lives. Which one was right?

Only time and God's grace could answer that question.

The phone rang, jarring Rory out of his thoughts. He answered it on the second ring.

"Hey, buddy, you and the boys want to go for Mexican?"

It was his friend Kip Lawrence. "Hey, Kip. The

boys are off with my sister. I'm on my own, but now that I think about it, I am hungry."

"Good. Penny abandoned me to go shopping—again," Kip replied, laughing. "I told her I might catch up with you since it's been a while. We need to plan a hunting trip."

"That sounds good," Rory said. "What time?"

"As soon as you can get to The Taco Mesa. I'm starving."

"I'll meet you there in fifteen minutes," Rory said, glad to have a friend tonight. "Thanks for calling."

He hung up, smiling. *Thanks to You, too, Lord, for getting me out of the house.*

He freshened up, then hurried to his truck, praying the whole time. Maybe if he prayed enough, he'd rid himself of his grief and guilt and all his erratic thoughts about Goldie Rios.

The Taco Mesa was booming tonight. All around them, people were laughing and eating. The bright, colorful Christmas lights lining the ceiling and walls illuminated the merriment in tiny spotlights of blue, yellow, red and green. Goldie had just bitten into her chips and hot sauce when she looked up and saw Rory walking in with another man.

"Oh, boy," she said, dropping her hand. There was no way to hide since they were seated in a booth right by the door.

"What is it?" Carla asked, glancing around to

where Rory stood waiting for a table. Then she shifted so fast she almost knocked over her water glass. "Is that him? Is that the famous nuisance hunter?"

"Shh," Goldie instructed on a low whisper. "He'll hear you."

Too late. Rory looked across the room and right at her. Caught, she could only wave and smile. "Oh, great. He's coming this way."

Goldie didn't know whether to be excited or sick to her stomach. She wanted to see Rory; she didn't want to see Rory. What was wrong with her? Since when had she become so indecisive and self-conscious?

Since she'd first woken up on his couch and seen that unforgettable face hovering over her like some knight in armor come to her rescue. Well, she didn't need rescuing now, did she?

No, but maybe the knight in question did. Because at this moment he looked about as anxious and confused as she felt. Even if he was smiling.

Chapter Nine

"Uh, hi."

Rory didn't know what else to say. He wondered if the good Lord was trying to hurry him into a relationship with Goldie or make him more patient. Either way, he was here and so was Goldie. And she looked great, except for the flush of surprise brightening her face. That flush actually made her look pretty, but the awkward frown accompanying it made Rory realize she probably felt as uncomfortable as he did right now. He hated making her feel that way but what was he supposed to do? Ignore her? That would be even worse.

"Hello." Her laughter was as brittle as the tortilla chips on the table. Then she waved a hand toward the redhead staring pointedly up at him. "Uh, Rory, this is my friend Carla McCoy. You've heard me mention her."

Rory nodded, extending his hand to Carla. "Yeah.

I think we talked on the phone once after Goldie's accident."

Carla shook his hand then smiled. "So you're the one who found her? The famous nuisance hunter?"

Rory put his hands in the pockets of his leather jacket. "Yeah. Good thing she found our house. It was a miserable night."

"Thank you for helping her," Carla said. "It's nice to meet you."

"You, too." Rory glanced back at Kip. "Well, I'm here with a buddy. Guess I'd better get back to him." He looked down at Goldie. "It's nice to see you again."

"Good to see you," she replied, her eyes going a deep green.

Before he could spin around and get away, Kip came over to the table. "Hey, Rory, Penny just called and she's finished shopping. Do you mind if she joins us for dinner?"

"No, I don't mind," Rory said. Then he looked back at Goldie. "This is my friend Kip Lawrence. We thought we'd grab a bite since my boys are with my sister and her kids. She's visiting my mom this weekend."

Kip nodded hello. "And my wife was out shopping," he interjected, laughing. "I guess she ran out of money."

Carla glanced from Rory to Goldie. "Well, since you're here and your wife is on the way, and we've all now been properly introduced, y'all want to sit with us?"

Goldie and Rory both spoke at the same time.

"I don't think—"

"Better not—"

Rory looked over at Kip. The gleam in Kip's eyes told him this wasn't going to be easy. Goldie's friend Carla had that same gleam. The let's-see-where-this-matchmaking-is-going gleam.

"Oh, c'mon," Carla pleaded. "I never get to meet any of Goldie's Viola friends. We don't mind, do we, Goldie?"

Rory watched as Goldie shifted and squirmed. She didn't want him to sit down with her, or maybe she did but she was afraid to say so. And he should just decline the invitation but he didn't want to do that, in spite of all his prayers to the contrary. "We don't want to interrupt," he offered, giving Goldie an out.

She shot her friend a stony glare then smiled up at him. "Y'all are welcome to eat with us, if Kip's wife won't mind."

"Are you kidding?" Kip replied. "She'll be glad for the female company. Besides, everyone in town's talking about how Rory here became a hero the night you had your wreck. She'd be mad as a wet hen if I passed up an opportunity to meet the woman Rory found on his couch."

Rory cringed then shrugged. "Sorry. I guess the word's gotten around, even if the story has taken on a life of its own."

Goldie lifted her eyebrows then looked at Kip. "Small-town grapevines have a tendency to embellish things, but yes, Rory did call 911 that night. And he's been a good friend since."

Kip slapped Rory on the back. "You're just that kind of guy, aren't you?"

"Yeah, I guess I am," Rory replied, wishing he'd stayed home and made a sandwich.

"All right then," Goldie replied. "It's settled. Just pull up some chairs and we'll get the waitress back over here."

Rory grabbed a chair from an empty table and swung it around so he'd be near Goldie. Might as well take advantage of this chance encounter. "You don't mind, really?" he said on a low tone for her ears only.

She gave him one of her famous Goldie looks. "No, I don't mind but..."

"But we're friends, Goldie. Just friends. So don't go all radar on me and look as if you'd like to bolt out the door."

She shook her head, her curls bouncing. "From the expression on your face, I thought maybe you were the one wanting to turn around and walk back out the door."

He smiled at that. "I did think about it."

They looked up to find Kip and Carla staring at them. Carla grabbed the bowl of chips and shoved them toward Kip. "Hey, I bet you've got pictures of your kids in your wallet. Let me see them."

Kip obliged but he grinned over at Rory while he fished out the pictures.

"I'm sorry." Goldie lowered her head as she gave her

friend a frown. "You have to understand, Rory's more used to saving me from bad situations than eating chips and hot sauce with me."

Kip lifted his head. "You mean there's more to this story?"

Goldie nodded. "I got trapped in a drainage ditch with a puppy a few days ago. Grams insisted Rory come over to help us out. Now I have a puppy named Spike and after I go back to Baton Rouge, Spike gets a new home with Rory and his boys."

"I love happy endings," Kip quipped with a hand to his heart. His grin made Goldie laugh but Rory thought about cuffing his friend on the ear.

Carla leaned forward. "You know, Goldie's always been accident-prone. We met in grammar school and when we both got new bikes for our birthdays, she took off on hers and had a wreck and broke her left arm." She shrugged. "Of course, a broken arm didn't stop her from riding her bike that summer. And from getting a skinned knee from yet another mishap." She grinned over at Goldie. "Then she moved away and came back later when we were in high school and we took up right where we'd left off. We got our driver's licenses together and—"

"And I promptly backed my mom's minivan into another car at the apartment complex where we lived," Goldie finished. "I think I was grounded for about a year after that."

"I had to do all the driving for a while," Carla

added. "Then they moved again and, well, no telling what kind of things she got into while they were away."

Rory laughed at that. "I'm glad Carla's here. She can update me on *all* your previous accidents. Or at least the ones she actually witnessed."

"Uh, not a good idea," Goldie said. "I wasn't that bad. And can we please change the subject?"

Carla ignored that plea then gleefully launched into childhood tales of daring deeds that had apparently gotten both of them in trouble.

In a few minutes, Kip did the same with Rory's past, telling the group grand tales of their adventures hunting, fishing and swimming all around the area. "Rory though, he always wanted to capture animals and release them back into the wild or take them to some animal preserve instead of just hunting them down for sport. He sure is in the right profession."

Kip looked up to find a leggy brunette grinning down at him. "Are you bragging about the adventures of Kip and Rory again?"

His eyes crinkled in a smile then he looked sheepish. "This is my lovely wife, Penny. Have a seat, honey."

Penny nudged Rory. "Good to see you. It's been a while."

"Yep." Rory introduced everyone and soon after the waitress rushed their orders through and brought the food out so they could finally eat.

Rory looked at Goldie, glad that the conversation

soon shifted from their personal lives to more current events and the upcoming holidays.

She looked just about as relieved as he did.

"That was nice," Goldie told Rory as they all stood outside the restaurant, the chill of the December night a sharp contrast to the warmth of the lively restaurant.

"It was," Rory replied, his eyes holding hers. "You know, we might be able to do this again, just the two of us, on a real date or something."

Goldie's pulse did a jagged little dance. "Are you sure about that? I mean, we did decide…"

"We didn't really decide anything except that we could be friends while you're here. And friendship never changes, right?"

She glanced over at Carla. Her friend was chatting with Kip and Penny as if they'd been friends forever.

"No, it doesn't." She wanted to be Rory's friend, but she wasn't sure how to do that. It seemed a letdown when she thought about all the other possibilities, but she did care about him and she liked being around him. Then she said something that surprised her. "I just don't have many male friends."

"Well, now's your chance to give it a try. You know, men are perfectly acceptable as friends. We've even been known to shed a tear or two during sappy movies."

"I do know that. It's just that in my case, I usually want more and it backfires and then I'm left alone again."

He leaned close. "I didn't leave you alone when I found you that night in my house, did I?"

She shook her head. "No."

"And I didn't leave you alone when I found you and Spike in that ditch, did I?"

"No, but you were just being you. Doing your job. You're that kind of man, Rory. The kind who rescues God's creatures."

"Sometimes, it's not that simple," he said. "Sometimes I have to take an animal down."

"Oh, well, then—"

"Relax. I've never taken down a woman before."

"You might be tempted if you stay around me long enough."

"I'll take my chances." He glanced over at their friends. "I'll call you next week, okay? We can spend time together and enjoy each other's company, nothing more unless we both feel ready to take that next step. No pressure."

"Okay." She shifted, stomping her boots against the pavement. It would be hard to honor that "no pressure" clause but she sure did want to try. "We'd better go. Grammy's by herself."

"I'll be in touch." He tipped his hand in farewell then turned to Kip and Penny. "I'm ready."

After goodbyes and some more ribbing, they parted ways. Goldie got into Carla's little economy car, huddling in her wool coat.

"He's adorable," Carla noted, cranking the car

and shivering while she waited for the heat to kick in.

"Adorable?" Goldie had to giggle at that.

"Well, yeah, in that rugged, outdoorsman-type way," Carla replied. "I mean, let's face it, girl, you usually go for the corporate-image type."

"Yes, and how's that been working for me?" Goldie quipped.

"I see your point." Carla whipped out into the scant traffic on the main street running through Viola, the flash of red and green illuminated wreaths on each streetlamp brightening their way. Across the square a huge palm tree sparkled with twinkling white lights, two giant synthetic snowmen grinning and looking just a bit out of place underneath the tropical tree. "Do you like him?"

"Of course I like him," Goldie admitted. "It's just that I don't see a future with him."

"Why not?"

"I have to get back to Baton Rouge, for starters. And I don't think he's the kind of man who would go for a long-distance relationship."

"It's not that far from Viola to Baton Rouge. Just hit I-10 and go east for about an hour, depending on traffic."

"I know the way," Goldie replied. "But I don't know the way into Rory's world. The man lost his wife to a violent crime and he has two little boys. He's a real family man."

"Wow."

She heard Carla's shivering intake of breath. "Yeah, wow. And the older son—Sam—he doesn't exactly want me in their life. But it's not about me. That little boy has a right to be mad at the world. He lost his mother." She leaned against the door. "And I lost my locket after the accident."

Carla held the steering wheel then glanced over at her. "You didn't tell me about that."

"I don't want to talk about it. I don't know where I lost it. I've looked in the spot where I had the wreck, searched my messed-up car at the garage and Rory's checked all over his house and yard. Someone could have taken it at the hospital, I just don't know."

"I'm sorry you lost your locket but what does that have to do with you and Rory?"

Goldie didn't know how to explain it. "It's just that Grams always told me the locket was special. She said it would bring good to me because it was so filled with love and family ties. And my daddy put the picture of me and him in there for that very reason. So I guess I set my high hopes on always having that locket as a security blanket or a reminder of all the good in the world. And now, it's gone. Grams said the locket isn't important—it's the love behind it that counts. It's the strength of the Lord's love that will bring the most good in my life."

She shrugged, knowing she could tell Carla anything. "It's silly, but I was sort of drifting before I came here to help Grams. I guess I'm getting restless in Baton Rouge. So I thought maybe a change of scenery would get me back on the right track. I still like my work and I've met my deadlines, even out of the office. But I just had this funny notion that if I left for a while maybe Loser Number Five would miss me enough to actually make a commitment. And instead, I find him buying a dog for another woman on the very night we're supposed to see each other for the first time in weeks. And then, I have this wreck and I lose my necklace."

"On the same night you find the perfect man—or rather, the perfect man finds you. I do see your dilemma, yeah."

Goldie heard the sarcasm in her friend's words. "I'm overanalyzing this, aren't I?"

Carla tapped the wheel. "Just a bit. And so because of all of the above and especially because you lost your locket, you think you can't be happy with Rory?"

Goldie bobbed her head. "I know it doesn't make sense but that necklace was my lifeline. I wanted to pass it on to my own daughter one day. And now it's out there somewhere, lost or sold or sitting in a pawn shop."

"Have you looked in any pawn shops?"

"We don't have one here, no."

"Oh, I guess that would be kind of fruitless, then."

"Yes and that's how I feel about Rory and a relationship—fruitless, pointless, end of discussion."

Carla pulled the car into the driveway behind Ruth's old sedan. "I never knew you were such a pessimist."

"I'm being realistic," Goldie replied, her pulse sounding an oncoming headache. "I just don't see how Rory and I can have any type of relationship other than friendship. It's not the right fit—he's not my type, I'm certainly not the stay-at-home-and-make-cookies type and we have different goals as far as our futures. I don't see how it can ever work."

Carla sat with her hands on the wheel, the car quiet now. "You don't think you're cut out to take on a man with two kids? Goldie, you're the queen of the organized life. You tell other woman how to handle everything from kids to animals to mothers-in-law and still maintain a perfect house. But you're not willing to take on all that yourself?"

"I guess not. I'm a big fraud, aren't I?"

"I didn't say that. I read your column and I've seen you in action. You know how to whip any room into shape and your advice is solid. In theory, at least."

"Well, in theory, I don't think I'm the woman for Rory, so there."

Carla bit her lower lip, deep in thought. "But would you like it to work?"

"I don't know," Goldie admitted. "I care about Rory and I'd like to get to know Sam and Tyler a little more. But his mother and he are close and I don't think she approves of me, either. It's just not the best situation to test my happily-ever-after skills. And besides, I'm still a little wounded by the incident at the mall and the spaghetti-in-his-lap breakup that followed."

"Sounds like you've found lots of excuses for not moving forward on this."

"Not excuses, realistic problems, Carla." Goldie didn't want to talk about it anymore. "Hey, what about you? You said you'd tell me everything about your new man."

"Yes, I said later when we did the girlie things."

"Well, let's go inside, don our PJs and get started," Goldie said, opening her door. "I need to concentrate on someone besides myself."

"Good," Carla replied. "Because I've been dying to tell you more but I wanted to wait until the right time." She got out of the car and came around to meet Goldie at the front door. "Goldie, I really think I've found the one. You know, when I said I think I've found the right man?"

"Yes, and I'd like to hear the whole story." Goldie eyed her friend then saw the glow surrounding Carla there in the porch light. "*The one?* Really?"

"Yes," Carla reiterated, clapping her hands together. "I think I'm in love, finally. But just like you, I'm afraid to admit that. I could mess up things, too."

Goldie took in that declaration and the doubt in her friend's words then stared at Carla. "First of all, you won't mess up. And second, why didn't you say something earlier? Besides, hey, I have to meet this man."

Carla put her hands on Goldie's arms. "I…I didn't want to rub it in since you've been so down."

Goldie saw the regret in her friend's eyes. "Don't be silly. You know I'm not that way. I'm happy for you, really."

But when she hugged Carla close, she had to work hard to put on a happy face so she could celebrate with her friend.

Because Goldie couldn't help but wonder why this kind of happiness couldn't happen for her, too. Maybe because you keep pushing it away, that voice in her head retorted.

Maybe so. But Rory did say he was going to call her.

That notion gave her the courage to stand back and smile at her friend. "Let's get inside so you can tell me everything. And I'll give you the best advice possible—on the house. And in theory, of course."

Chapter Ten

The next morning, Goldie awoke to her cell phone ringing. Turning, she grabbed the humming device while trying to fully wake up. She and Carla had stayed up half the night talking about men, just like they used to do in high school talking about boys.

"Hello," she said in a dry-throated whisper.

"Goldie, thank goodness you're there. I need help."

"Rory?" Hearing the panicked sound of his voice brought Goldie fully alert. "What's wrong?"

"It's my mom," he said. "My sister just called. They're rushing her to the hospital. Becky thinks she had a heart attack."

"Oh, no."

Goldie glanced over at Carla. Her friend lay in the bed with one eye open then mouthed, "What?"

"It's Rory," Goldie explained with a hand to her phone as she sat up on the bed. "What can I do to help?"

"Becky and I need to be at the hospital but we don't have anyone to leave the kids with. Could you...?"

"I'll be there as soon as I can," Goldie replied.

"Thanks. I couldn't think of anyone else. Most of my mom's friends aren't good with this many young children. And I couldn't get anyone else on the phone—everyone's out Christmas shopping. I...I thought at least the boys kinda know you."

"I'll be there," she promised. "I'll bring Carla with me. She comes from a big family, so she's used to lots of kids."

"Good. I'll send Becky on behind the ambulance then I'll wait for y'all."

Goldie hung up then whirled around to Carla. "You have to come with me." She quickly described the situation. "I don't know a thing about entertaining little boys."

Carla got up, pushing at her hair. "Well, we'll figure it out together. They mostly like to eat and fight and throw balls—stuff like that. Don't worry."

But Goldie was worried. About Rory and his mom. If something happened to Mrs. Branagan—she didn't want to think about that right now. Spike came bouncing into the room then hopped up on the bed. "Maybe we should take you, too," Goldie added as she went about combing her hair and getting on her jeans and a sweater. "Dogs and boys just naturally go together, don't they?" And the boys needed to adjust to Spike if they were going to adopt him after Christmas.

Carla nodded then yawned, her sleepy eyes like two slits. "We shouldn't have stayed up half the night gabbing."

Goldie was wide-awake. "Too late to worry about that. I'll make coffee once we get to Rory's."

Grams came to the door. "What's wrong?"

Goldie told her the news on her way to the bathroom. "Grams, you might want to alert the prayer warriors at church."

"I sure will," Grams said. "Do you want me to come along?"

Goldie almost said no then turned. "Would you like to? I mean, just so I don't worry about you if I have to stay all day? We'll take both cars and that way, if you get tired, Carla can bring you home."

"Of course," Grams declared. "I'm already dressed and I've had all my medication. Just let me gather a few things. I can sit at Rory's house same as here, I reckon. Or better yet, we'll make some soup for later. They'll all need their nourishment."

Goldie nodded then hurried away. When she came back into the bedroom, Carla looked up at her. "He trusts you with his children," she noted. "I think that must mean something."

Goldie shook her head. "He panicked. I haven't been around them that much. I was the first person he thought about."

"Exactly," Carla said, her smug expression belying the seriousness of that one word.

"After he'd tried calling other people," Goldie replied, throwing on a heavy sweater and warm booties.

"Still, you were high up on the list, apparently."

Goldie wasn't sure how to take that. What did Rory normally do in such an emergency? Who would he have called if she hadn't been available? Maybe he'd never had such an emergency before. He did depend on his mother a lot whenever he was called away, but she'd never heard him mention any other babysitters.

Well, now he's beginning to depend on you, too, she thought. Maybe Carla had a point.

Grams materialized with her walker and a big tote bag in the attached basket. "I think Carla's right, honey. Rory respects you and he knows you'll take care of things for him."

Goldie heard the hopeful tone in Grammy's voice. "Your hearing sure is intact," she said, searching for her purse.

"And so is my eyesight," Grams replied with a serene smile. "It's all gonna be all right. God is always in control."

Carla grabbed Spike, holding him close. "That's right. Grams knows these things."

"I just hope Mrs. Branagan is all right," Goldie murmured. "Now let's go."

Goldie helped Grams into her car and waited as Carla backed out first so she could follow. Spike barked at Carla's car as they passed.

Goldie said the same prayer over and over. *Let her*

be okay, dear Lord. She couldn't think beyond that. She'd help Rory, no doubt, no questions asked. As for the meaning behind his request, it was simple, really. He'd been worried about his mother, nothing else.

And yet, her heart burned with a strange warm, sappy emotion in spite of her cynical nature. Rory had called on her to rescue him this time.

That was sure a first.

"I'm sorry," Rory apologized, ushering Goldie and her little troupe into the house. "I just didn't know where else to turn." He waved a hand in the air. "The house is a mess. The boys are getting dressed and Becky's girls are watching cartoons. I've explained things to them, but it's just not good."

"It's okay," Goldie said, seeing the glaze of worry in his eyes. "Just go and be with your mom. Grams and Carla will be here to make sure I don't blow up the oven or flood the house."

That almost brought a smile to his face. "All right. I'd better hurry. I've left numbers on a pad on the counter, just in case. And you have my cell number."

"Go," she ordered, pushing him toward the back door.

"Rory, we'll be praying," Grams said, giving him a hug.

"Thanks, to all of you." He gave Goldie one last look then headed out the door.

Carla glanced toward the den. "I'll go see how the girls are doing."

Spike squirmed out of Grammy's arms then headed down the hallway, barking.

Two bedroom doors opened wide as both boys came rushing out.

"Spike!" Tyler's eyes, so like his father's, gleamed with delight. "Hey, Sam, Spike's here."

Sam looked up at the three women and reached down to pet Spike then turned back toward his room. Goldie decided she'd have to be the one to handle this. It was now or never for her and Sam. And she so wanted to make it work.

"Hey, Tyler, my friend Carla says she wants to make some cookies. Can you help her find stuff in the kitchen?"

Tyler bobbed his head. "Can Spike come?"

"Sure." Goldie watched as the puppy skidded up the hallway behind the little boy.

Grams nodded. "Go ahead. I'll go get to know Becky's girls."

Goldie glanced around the house, seeing it with new eyes since Rory's mom hadn't been here to clean. The hall tree by the back door was cluttered with sports equipment and muddy sneakers. Book bags lay open and grinning right by the shoes. Jackets and coats of all sizes and shapes lay piled like hay bales on the walnut bench seat and on top of every available bit of space. Dirty dishes lined the counter. A cereal box sat bent and open right by the forgotten milk. She hurriedly put away the milk and closed and put away the cereal. She'd tackle the rest later.

This place does need a woman's touch, she thought. Rory's mother did her best but now that effort might have caught up with her. Goldie closed her eyes and asked God to take care of all of them.

Then she went to Sam's bedroom door and knocked. "Sam, it's Goldie. May I come in?"

No answer.

She tried again, tapping gently against the wood. "Sam, I just want to talk to you."

Finally, the door crept open and Sam stood there, the expression on his face somewhere between pouting and defiant. "I'm okay."

Goldie inched the door open then surveyed the room. It held the standard bunk beds and sports posters, a bookcase and a basket full of various balls. Clothes, shoes and books cluttered the floor. Goldie picked up a black and white soccer ball. "Do you play soccer?"

He nodded then plopped down on his unmade bed. Goldie itched to straighten the room but knew that would be a mistake. "And I guess you play baseball, too, huh?"

Another nod. And then words so quiet, she almost didn't hear them. "My mom used to come to all my games."

That simple statement almost broke Goldie's heart. How could she fault this kid for his attitude? He'd lost his mother when he was still so young. How horrible that must have been for them. Goldie thought of her own mother and suddenly felt the urge to hug Angela close, flaws and all. She wished Angela would come home for Christmas so she could just talk to her, at least.

"I bet your mother was sure proud of you."

Sam didn't respond. He just sat there staring at the bookshelf. Goldie sat silent, wishing she knew what to say.

"Is my Grandma gonna die?" he finally asked, his head down.

How should she answer that? Deciding to be honest, Goldie cleared her throat. "I don't know. Your dad will call us and let us know what the doctors say. But I'm going to hope and pray that your grandmother will be all right. You can do that, too, you know. It's okay to say a prayer."

He looked at her then, his big eyes devoid of any kind of hope. "My mom died. It was too late to pray for her."

Goldie had to restrain herself from gathering him close. "I know, honey. That was a hard blow. A terrible thing." She sat still, not daring to reach out. "There's just no easy way to deal with that, is there?"

He shook his head. "I miss her."

"I'm sure you do."

"I don't want Grandma to die," he said. He turned to stare up at Goldie. "I'm sorry."

Goldie wanted to take him into her arms and

reassure him that it would be all right. For the first time in her life, her maternal instincts kicked in and went into full-power mode. And she knew at that moment, if she ever had a child of her own, she would protect that child with a fierce heart. But right now, she wanted to protect *this* child.

"Don't be sorry for being honest, Sam. None of us likes seeing people we love die. I was so worried about my Grams when she fell and broke her hip. Grams is this amazing woman who knows that we have everlasting life after death—eternal life with God."

Sam shifted away. "No, you don't understand," he pleaded, his voice rising.

Goldie tried again. "But I do—"

He got up, fisted his hands. "I'm not talking about that. I don't want Grandma to die but you don't know—Dad doesn't know what happened. I did something really bad."

Goldie's heart started beating triple time. "What do you mean?"

"It's my fault," Sam confessed. "I caused Grandma to have the heart attack. I know it was my fault."

Rory stood by the doors to the ICU, watching as doctors and nurses rushed by. No one had come to talk to him and Becky yet and his sister was beside herself.

"We should hear something soon," he said, reassuring her for about the tenth time.

Becky nodded. "I still can't believe it. One minute

we were standing there wrapping gifts. I left the room to check on the kids—the girls were fighting as usual—and when I walked back in, she started clutching her chest and then she fell to the floor. I was only gone about five minutes. I was so scared. I tried to talk to her but she wasn't making any sense. She couldn't speak. It was horrible."

"I'm just glad you were there with her," Rory said, closing his eyes, his hand on his sister's arm. "I don't get it, either. She's always been so healthy. Dad was the one we had to watch and worry about."

"*She* watched and worried," Becky replied. "Maybe it's catching up with her. First Rachel's death and then Dad. It's hard for any of us to bear."

Rory nodded. "She took both hard. We all did. And then, I started depending on her way too much."

Becky put her hand over his. "You've done a good job with the boys, Rory. Anyone can see that."

"Mom helped a lot, though," he said. "I leaned on her too much. I didn't want to take advantage of her and I should have just hired a sitter right away, so we could adjust, but you know Mom. She insisted everything was fine. I should have insisted—"

Becky shook her head. "No, Mom wanted to help. She loves the boys. If I'd let her, she'd have the girls here half the time, too."

He smiled at that. "Yeah, I guess we can't beat ourselves up for this, but I just don't know what provoked her into having a heart attack—if it was a heart attack."

Becky shook her head. "I've always heard heart attacks are like a silent killer among women."

Rory glanced down the hall. "I wish the doctor would come out here and tell us what's happening."

Becky glanced at the buzzing cell phone in her hand. "That's William. I'd better give him an update."

Rory watched as his sister poured out her heart to her husband then assured him that he didn't need to drive all the way from Dallas to be there. "Just wait until I have more information," Becky said. "I might need to stay here a while longer and you'll need to come and get the girls if I do."

Rory thought back over the night he'd gotten the call about Rachel. He couldn't even remember getting to the hospital, couldn't remember his mother taking the boys out of the room so he could tell his dying wife goodbye. He just remembered seeing Rachel lying there, so pale and so still…and then she was gone. Just like that.

Things could certainly change in a heartbeat. He knew that firsthand. He'd seen that firsthand. He thought about Goldie and how she'd come into his life and again, he thanked God that she had found warmth and comfort in his house that night.

Goldie.

She'd made it through. And for some strange reason she'd made it into his life. Today, he'd thought of her when he needed help. But had he been wrong to call on her, to depend on Goldie to help him?

Or had he been right? Exactly right?

Rory didn't have the answers to his own questions and right now, he could only take a breath and thank God that Goldie had come through for him. He wouldn't forget it. He'd make it up to her when this was all over. And he wouldn't waste precious time wondering what was wrong or right or how to handle the complications.

He'd just enjoy the gift God had shown him. The gift of finding hope again.

Then he looked up to find Becky waiting for him, her phone silent now.

"Rory, the doctor wants to talk to us. It wasn't a heart attack. It was a stroke."

Chapter Eleven

Goldie sat staring out at the gray winter day, glad she'd done most of her Christmas shopping. Today was the last Saturday before Christmas. If she had to spend it inside, at least Rory's house was nice and warm.

And clean now, thanks to Carla and Goldie.

They'd cleaned, baked, made soup—Grams insisted on soup, of course. And now they were waiting for the biscuits Carla had whipped up to rise and brown. Rory could come home to a good, hearty supper and a warm, sparkling-clean house.

If they could just keep the four kids from messing it up again.

Carla was at the kitchen counter talking quietly on her cell phone with her new man. Tyler was asleep on his bed after helping with the cookies and the biscuits, Spike curled up by his side. The girls were sprawled on the den floor by the fire, reading books and listening to their separate headphones and Sam…well, Sam was still in his room. He had come out a few times—to eat, help clean up, play with Spike and stare up at Goldie, his heart in his eyes. And his future in her hands.

Goldie now knew why he was so sure he'd caused his grandmother's attack. But she couldn't tell anyone. She'd promised Sam. She'd also urged him to tell his dad the truth. Why the boy had decided to trust her, of all the other people in this house, was beyond Goldie's comprehension, but he had. And she thanked God he had, while she tried to understand his reasoning.

Now, the question remained. Would the child do the right thing and tell his father the truth?

"What's wrong, honey?"

Goldie glanced up to find Grams hovering nearby on her souped-up walker. The tennis balls on the base of the walker's legs added traction and the garland of berries and red flowers looping around the basket added holiday festivity. Becky's daughters had insisted on decorating the walker to give it some Christmas cheer.

But right now, Gram's didn't seem to be in a festive mood, in spite of the sweet smile on her face. And because she knew that smile meant business, Goldie answered, "Nothing. Just worried."

"Are you hungry?"

Goldie looked up at her Grammy, love filling her heart to the breaking point. "No, Grams. After a sandwich, three oatmeal cookies and two cups of coffee, I'm good until dinnertime."

"Okay. Do you want to talk?"

"About what?"

"About Rory and your feelings for him."

"I don't have feelings for him."

"Oh, yes, you do."

Goldie glanced around to make sure they were alone and that the girls still had their music piped into their ears. "Grams, what are you talking about?"

"I told you, I'm not blind. I saw it the minute Rory brought you home from the hospital. And I'm not completely deaf even if I do have to wear a hearing aid now and then. I hear it in your voice and in his. You two have something stewing, that's for sure."

Goldie couldn't deny it. "I care about Rory. He's a nice man—"

"It's more than that," Grams said. "I've never known you to go out on a limb for anyone other than family, child. But you didn't hesitate this morning. You came to Rory's aid and you've done a good job of corralling all of us here today. It must be love, or at least the beginning of love."

Goldie closed her eyes to find patience. "Grams, you can't go around saying things like that. It's complicated. Rory is a friend and he needed us."

Grams backed up to sit in the chair across from

Goldie. "I'm not announcing it on the evening news, so don't worry. Complicated? How so?"

Goldie waved a hand in the air. "Look around. The man has two children and a mother who's sick. And he's a widower."

Grams slanted her eyebrows. "Your point?"

Goldie leaned close to whisper. "My point is—I'm not cut out to be an instant mother and the man's still grieving his wife. Besides, with his mother being sick now, he's going to have a whole lot to deal with and right here before Christmas. I don't think he'll be in the mood to woo me."

"But it's the perfect time for you to be a good friend to him."

Goldie tried to be patient. "I'm doing that right now."

Grams sat silent for a minute, gazing at the fire, the picture of innocence. Then she patted the arm of her chair as if following the beat of some silent song. "Do you want to be wooed?"

Goldie knew her grandmother could be stubborn since she'd inherited that same trait, but she sure didn't know the woman could be so intuitive. Grams had read her very heart. But Goldie wasn't ready to concede that fact.

"I don't know," she admitted. "I make a mess of relationships. I've been through a lot of bad ones lately."

"Maybe because you've been looking for love in all the wrong places," Grams quipped.

"That's my life," Goldie shot back. "Like the lyrics of a country song."

"Country songs are deeply rooted in real-life feelings. You should listen to the local station more often. That and our wonderful gospel station."

"I'll make a note," Goldie teased, giving her grandmother an impish grin. Then she leaned back in her chair. "Sam has some issues and I don't know how to handle that."

"You talked to the boy earlier," Grams reminded her. "What came of that?"

"I promised him I'd keep that between him and me," Goldie replied. "I have to honor that promise, but I did urge him to talk to his dad."

"Trying to win his trust—that's a good start."

"No, just trying to stay out of things," Goldie said, even though what Sam had told her put her square in the middle of a bad situation. What should she do?

Again, Grams seemed to read her thoughts. "Prayer, darlin'. Prayer will bring answers."

"Is it truly that easy?" Goldie asked, wanting with all her soul to be as sure as her grandmother. "I do pray but it seems so halfhearted and I seem to pray only in emergencies."

Grams shook her head. "Being a Christian isn't supposed to be easy, honey. But prayer brings comfort and answers—answers that the Lord knows are already in our hearts. We just have to get clarity and prayer helps with that, but you have to rely on God's strength during both good and bad times, not just as a last resort."

"So, you think God listens to each and every prayer?"

"Of course I do. God's arms are wide open enough for everyone, even you." She winked. "And so are mine."

Goldie leaned over to kiss her grandmother. "I'll keep that in mind, too, Grams." Then she whispered, "Do you ever pray for Mama? Do you ever pray that she'll come home just to see if we're both okay?"

Ruth's lips twisted in a frown. "Every day, honey. I'm stubborn that way. Even though your mother and I are worlds apart, I still love her. I love her because she loved my son and their love brought me you and that's reason enough to easily forgive her ways."

"Grams, you amaze me," Goldie said, grinning. "I'm gonna pray for her, too. It can't hurt."

"That's for sure."

The phone rang and Goldie rushed to get it. Carla came into the den, her own phone in her hand. She closed it, watching Goldie.

"Hey, it's me," Rory said.

He sounded so drained. "Hey. Any word?"

"Yes, but it's not good. She's suffered a mild stroke but the doctors say she should have a full recovery. It was a TIA—transient ischemic attack—I think is the official term. They think she's had several over the last few months and this was probably the worst. No permanent damage since we got her to the hospital so quickly, and thankfully, she takes an aspirin every morning anyway, so that probably helped. But the chance of a second stroke is high, so they want to keep her in the hospital and on medication for now. She might need some therapy—something about comprehension and memory. They're going to do a few more tests and get her on the right medicine and a new diet."

Goldie wished she could say something to make him feel better. "Rory, I'm so sorry. But I'm so glad you acted quickly this morning. Listen, just stay there as long as you need. Everything is fine here."

"Are you sure? Becky and I were talking and one of us can come home to relieve y'all."

"Maybe later," Goldie said. "Just stay there with your mom for now. Grams sent Carla to the store and we've been baking and cooking all afternoon. We have vegetable-beef soup for supper and also cookies and biscuits." She didn't tell him that she'd scrubbed down the kitchen, washed three loads of clothes and pretty much reorganized the whole pantry.

"And the kids?"

Goldie thought about Sam. Rory didn't need to worry about that right now. "They're all okay. Settled down and cozy. We're going to wrap some gifts later."

"I need to finish my shopping," he replied on a sigh. "Christmas is just a few days away. But Mom's gonna need both Becky and me for a while."

"I can help with that, too."

"Goldie, I can't expect you to do everything. I've been doing it all for a long time now. I mean, Mom helped a lot…."

He stopped. The silence spoke of his pain.

While Goldie hid her own. But this wasn't about her hurt feelings at hearing him snap at her. His frustration wasn't toward her, after all. "She's going to be okay, Rory."

"You know you can't promise that." He went silent then said, "I'm sorry. I'm just tired and worried."

"I understand."

"I think you truly do, Goldilocks. You've been through this kind of stuff yourself with your grandmother."

"Grams said we need to pray and I'm gonna listen to her. She's very wise, you know."

"She's the best," he replied. "Thank her for me. And, Goldie, when things are better, I intend to take you out—just the two of us. To thank *you*."

"That sounds nice, but not necessary," she said, wondering why she'd said that. But it was true—a date with Rory sounded wonderful—and the first step was admitting she was drawn to this man.

"Good. I'll hold you to that. I just hope everything goes okay with Mom."

"It will, Rory. I don't know your mother that well, but she strikes me as a strong, determined woman. And she's still young enough to recover."

"You're right there. She's tough."

"So you have to be tough, too. And don't worry about us. We're fine. Stay there as long as you need to."

"Thanks. I feel better knowing everything's okay back home. I'll keep you posted."

She hung up, her thoughts on Frances and her recovery. Then she thought of Sam. After giving Grams and Carla a report about Rory's mom, she said, "Grams, I'm going to check on Tyler and Spike and see how Sam's doing. He might be persuaded with another one of Carla's cookies to come out of his room again. And he'll want to know about his grandmother."

"Good idea, honey. I think I'll just recline here on this nice, soft couch and get a few winks."

Carla nodded then whisked the girls up. "Hey, how about a nature walk?"

"It's cold out there," the oldest one remarked.

"Good for you to get some fresh air," Carla replied. "Let's look at natural stuff to make a holiday centerpiece. And while we walk, I'll explain about what happened to your grandmother. She's going to be fine, but you need to know what to expect."

That seemed to do the trick. The girls ran toward the door, throwing on jackets and hats as they went.

Goldie guided her grandmother over to the couch. "Lie down. I'll wrap this blanket around you."

Grams leaned against the pillows, causing Goldie to remember she'd ruined one of them the night of her accident. Making a note to get a new one for Rory for

Christmas, at least, she found the plaid comforter and put it over Grams's legs. "Rest."

Grams smiled, already drowsy. "I'll pray myself to sleep."

Goldie did a little more tidying, fluffing pillows and picking up magazines. She could hear Carla laughing with the girls in the backyard as she talked about her boyfriend. Goldie wanted to feel jealous, but she didn't have it in her heart to be that way. Carla deserved a good man, someone to love.

And maybe she did, too. But first, she needed to see how Sam was doing. She headed down the short hallway then tapped on the door. When she didn't get a response, she carefully opened the door, thinking maybe he was already in bed. But the room was empty and Sam was nowhere to be found.

Goldie turned and went across the hall to Tyler's room. He was fast asleep but Spike saw her and bounced off the bed.

"C'mon, boy," she said. "We need to find Sam."

Where had the boy gone? Was he hiding out because of what he'd done? Or had he run away from home, hoping to spare himself from having to confess to his father?

I can't call Rory, she thought. She'd just look around the house and yard. Maybe Sam had gone outside. But she would have seen him coming through the house since both the front and back doors were in plain sight of the open den and kitchen.

Tyler was safe and Grams was dozing. Goldie grabbed her jacket and stepped into the backyard, motioning to Carla. Spike headed toward the girls, barking playfully. "I can't find Sam," she said softly so the girls couldn't hear. They were busy breaking magnolia leaves from a nearby tree.

"What?" Carla brushed at her hair.

"Sam isn't in his room. Have you seen him out here?"

"No, but we only made it as far at this tree. We're going to spray these leaves gold."

"That's great, but I have to find Sam."

"Oh, of course. What should I do with the girls?"

Goldie glanced over at Lauren and Regina. "Hey, you two, have you seen Sam anywhere out here?"

"No, ma'am," they both answered. Spike barked his own reply. "He's pouting."

"He's not in his room," Goldie replied, walking toward them. "Did he tell you why he was mad?"

Lauren shook out the shiny green leaves she'd gathered. "Sam's a little rude. He never smiles. I don't know what's wrong with him."

Goldie shot a glance toward Lauren. "He's just confused and…he misses his mother. And now his grandmother is sick. Cut him some slack, okay?"

Regina twirled around. "Is Grandma gonna be all right?"

Carla nodded. "Yes, we think. Remember I explained she'd had a tiny stroke. She's in good hands and the doctors know exactly what kind of treatment to give her. She just might need to take it easy for a while."

"Will she be home for Christmas?"

"We hope so," Goldie offered, unsure what to say next.

Carla pushed at Goldie. "Go look for Sam and I'll take care of these two. I'll watch for him." Then she whistled at Spike. "C'mon, boy. Let's play in the leaves."

Goldie hurried down the long driveway, searching through the cypress trees and old oaks, calling Sam's name as she went. She checked in the storage shed behind the house and down by the bayou. She walked out onto the short pier and stared into the woods and out into the dark water. Was Sam doing this deliberately since he'd confessed all to her earlier? Was he afraid of being punished?

I told him he'd have to be the one to tell his dad the truth, Goldie reminded herself. Why would he bolt now?

Then Goldie reached into the pocket of her jeans and pulled out her returned locket, her fingers rubbing against the tiny porcelain frame.

"Where are you, Sam?"

How in the world could she explain his son's disappearance to Rory if Sam didn't show up? How could she tell him that Sam had found her locket the night she'd had her wreck and that the boy had been hiding it since then?

And that his grandmother had discovered the missing locket this morning right before she'd had her stroke.

Chapter Twelve

After calling Sam's name over and over, Goldie went back into the house. The sun was going down, the chill of early evening causing her to shiver as she knocked dirt off her boots. She'd have some major work to catch up on when she got home tonight. But right now, she wasn't too worried about that. And in spite of all the new and exciting things happening all around her—things she couldn't explain—she now had a better perspective on how to answer a lot of the questions she got. That would make her editor at the paper happy. Firsthand experience always provided the best resource.

But Goldie would keep most of what she'd learned dealing with Rory and his sons to herself for now. It was too personal to share in an advice column.

Getting back to finding Sam, she hurried through the house.

Grams was up and watching an old movie. "There you are. Everything all right?"

"Have you seen Sam?" Goldie asked, praying the boy was somewhere in the house.

"No, but then I just woke up a few minutes ago. You can't find him?"

"No, and I've looked all over the yard and even in the woods. I'm getting concerned but I don't want to call Rory."

"Are you sure you've looked everywhere? Young boys can hide out in the oddest of places. Your father used to do that a lot."

Goldie backtracked in her mind. "Everywhere but the master bedroom." She walked over to the sofa. "Do you think I should look in there?"

"I would," Grams replied. "I can't imagine why he'd be in there, but maybe he figured that would be the one place no one would look."

"Good point," Goldie said, heading down the hallway toward the back of the long house. Since the door to Rory's room had been closed before, she hadn't gone in there and she hadn't allowed anyone else to do so, either. But now, she didn't have a choice.

She didn't bother knocking. Instead, she carefully opened the door and stared into the dark room, her eyes adjusting to the late-afternoon shadows. And there on the floor sat Sam. The boy had pictures strewn all around him.

"Sam, didn't you hear me calling you?" Goldie

asked, wondering if she was able to help this troubled child.

Sam glanced up and shrugged, his eyes big and solemn. "I'm sorry. I didn't want anyone to know where I was."

Goldie let out a sigh of relief. "Well, you had me worried sick. I was just about to call your father."

Sam looked down at his hands. "I'm not supposed to be in here."

"I see. So I guess this is one more thing we're not going to tell him." She sank down on the floor beside him, her gaze skimming the haphazard bed linens and the masculine clothes scattered around the big room. She caught sight of a dainty jewelry box sitting open on the dresser, its baubles frozen in time. Averting her eyes, she told Sam, "You know something, you can't keep doing this. Your daddy loves you and he's got a lot to deal with right now. You could be a big help to him if you'd just try to talk to him. And if you can't do that, then maybe you need to talk to someone else to make you feel better."

Sam finally looked right at her. "You didn't tell him about the locket?"

"I told you I wouldn't," she repeated, wishing she could figure this child out. "You have to, though. He needs to know what you did and why you did it." She'd like to know that herself.

Sam's gaze held a mixture of trepidation and defiance. "He'll be mad at me. He's always mad at me."

Shocked to hear that, Goldie picked up one of the

pictures and saw the image of Sam's mother staring back at her. Rachel had been a pretty woman. She could see Rachel's eyes whenever she looked at Sam. "Why does he seem mad at you?"

"I don't know. He just doesn't talk to me very much. I wish he'd talk about Mom more, but I don't want to make him sad."

Goldie couldn't imagine this little boy's pent-up pain. "Maybe you just need to ask him about her. He might not realize you need to hear things about her."

"I can't."

Goldie decided to try another tactic. "Can you tell me why you took my necklace?"

He shifted through some pictures then tossed them back in a box. "I don't know. I found it by the couch and I just didn't know what to do with it."

"Did you know your daddy was looking for it?"

He nodded his head. "I was afraid I'd get in trouble for not showing it to him right away, so I didn't say anything. Is that a sin?"

Goldie needed someone much wiser to answer that question, but right now, Sam only had her. "It's a sin to lie, yes. But technically, you didn't lie. You just withheld information. So maybe it is a sin. Any way you look at it, it's not good. You need to come clean."

"Then I'll feel better?"

"You should. Your dad loves you and he's not going to hurt you. He might punish you but in the end, he'll be proud that you did the right thing."

He looked back at the pictures. "I thought maybe I could take the locket and put it on her grave—for a Christmas gift. Christmas isn't as fun as it used to be."

Goldie's heart shattered. This little boy had a whole lot going on underneath those thick bangs. "That's a nice thought but your mom wouldn't want a stolen locket on her grave. And, Sam, she wants you to have fun at Christmas. She wants you to laugh and play. You're a little boy—you've got a lot to laugh about."

He looked back at his mom's picture. "I want Daddy to laugh, too."

"But he does, doesn't he?"

"Some. But it's kind of fake, I think."

Goldie felt her legs going numb from sitting there crossed-legged but she couldn't move. "Well, let's think about this. Putting a necklace that doesn't belong to you on your mother's grave sure won't make him any happier, now will it?"

"I didn't do it, anyway. I was afraid he'd see it and be really mad. I hid it and then Grandma found it in that bag where I'd put it and then she got all upset and dizzy."

Goldie watched his face, saw how hard he was fighting his emotions. "Sam, you didn't cause your grandmother to get sick. It was something inside her, something already not right. She had a very light stroke but she has good doctors and she's going to need medicine and some therapy. But you can't pull any more tricks like this, okay? She doesn't need that kind of stress."

"So it *is* my fault?"

Goldie wanted to sink into the floor. "No, no. I just mean she has to take things easy so it would be nice if you didn't…,if you could… I think you need to let your dad explain what needs to be done."

He sat silent, staring at the pile of pictures. "Do you hate me?"

Goldie shook her head. "Of course not. I want to be your friend and I'm so proud of you for confiding in me about the necklace. You know, in a weird way, you've given me such a wonderful gift." She took the necklace out of her pocket and put it around her neck, her fingers brushing over it. "This necklace is very special to me because it has a picture of me and my dad inside. I lost my dad when I was young, so I know how you feel."

He gave her a doubtful look. "I saw the picture. Did you cry when he died?"

"Yes, a lot. My mom and I both did."

"My dad cried at the funeral. I remember. I cried, too. Tyler was too little. Grandma held him all day."

Goldie shut her eyes to the image of what that poignant memory must have been like. "I remember my mom crying at my daddy's funeral, too. That's tough to watch." Then she reached out a hand to Sam, hoping the boy would respond. "You know it's okay to cry, don't you?"

He pushed away. "I'm not a baby."

"Crying has nothing to do with being a baby," she

explained. "It hurts when someone we love dies. Tears are God's way of allowing us to be sad. But tears also allow us to heal our hearts, too."

He went into withdrawal again. Goldie had to wonder if Rory even knew how bad things were with his oldest son. She'd have to talk to him about this, somehow. But right now she had to think of something to bring Sam out of his self-imposed shell. Picking up one of the pictures, she said, "Hey, I have a great idea. Have you ever done any scrapbooking?"

Sam balked at that. "That sounds stupid."

"You don't even know what I'm talking about," she retorted, her tone playful. "But if you want to do something special for both your parents, we could make a weatherproof picture to put on your mom's grave and we could make something very special for your dad and your grandmother for Christmas. A scrapbook is like a picture book, but we'd add little things and maybe write something special by some of the pictures. And it can be just from you. A present from Sam. How about that?"

He acted unimpressed for a few seconds. Then he said, "Will you help me?"

"I'd love to," Goldie replied, her hand still near his. She wasn't sure when she'd get this done but she'd find the time. "It'll be a big surprise." Then she nodded her head. "I'll explain to your dad that I need to borrow you for a couple of hours one night next week, okay? That way he won't think I've kidnapped you or something."

Sam didn't say anything but he finally took her hand, shaking it as if they'd just made a business deal. "Will Spike be there?"

"Of course. He'll probably want to chew on a few of my scrapbook pages."

"Okay."

"Okay, then." Goldie closed her eyes for a minute, thanking God for allowing her to help this lost little boy.

And when she opened her eyes, Sam was actually smiling.

Rory went in to see his mother before going home.

"Hi," he said, taking her hand.

Frances gave him a drowsy smile. "Hi."

She could talk; that was a good sign. The doctors had explained she might have to deal with some memory loss and relearn her thought processes.

"Mom, I'm going home to check on the boys and Becky's girls. Becky's staying here tonight."

Frances shook her head. "Both go home. Now."

Seeing her struggle with her thoughts broke Rory's heart. "But—"

"No but. Go." Then she raised her eyebrows. "Who's with children?"

"Goldie and Miss Ruth."

At first, Frances looked confused, her expression twisting as if she were in pain. Then she settled back with a sigh. "That girl—"

"Yes, Mom. That girl. She's been great about this. And she's been with the kids all day long."

Frances smiled lopsidedly at that. "Make or break."

Rory understood what she was saying. "If she can survive a day with the boys, will you cut her some slack?"

Frances moved her head in a tiny nod. "Might."

Rory laughed at that, feeling better. "Thanks, Mom. I'll go talk to Becky and see if I can convince her to go home with me."

"Do it."

Rory had to laugh again. Even from a hospital bed, with wires attached to her, his mother was still barking orders and being firm. That attitude would help her to recover, he hoped. He prayed.

"Wait."

He turned at his mother's soft call. "Do you need something? Are you in pain?"

She shook her head. "Don't want…to be…pushed aside."

Rory saw the single tear moving down his mother's face. "You won't be pushed aside, Mom. You know how much we all depend on you. But you do need to get well."

She squinted. "Goldie."

"What about Goldie?"

"I didn't like her…taking over."

Rory suddenly understood. "Mom, she's not taking over. We're just friends and right now, neither of us is sure where that might lead. You need to rest and get better. Don't worry about Goldie."

"Not worried anymore."

Rory watched, amazed, as his mother managed a weak smile. "Go home."

"Yes, ma'am." His mother had given him her blessings. And in spite of worrying about her health, he felt as if a great weight had been lifted off his shoulders.

After telling Becky about their talk and convincing her to leave with him, Rory waited until his sister had told Frances good-night. Becky followed him home in her car, planning on picking up the girls to take them back to Frances's house.

When he pulled up to the house, Rory felt a gush of warmth seeping into his cold bones. The Christmas tree was sparkling just inside the window. Soft lighting flowed throughout the house, making it seem homey and welcoming. He stopped, his hands on the steering wheel.

It had been such a long time since he'd just sat looking at his house. This had been Rachel's dream house and he'd been heavily involved in building it. His dad had helped and so had several of his friends. After they'd moved in, she'd fussed and fixed and made it a home.

But the day she died, all the warmth had left this house. Rory had tried so hard to keep things the way she'd want them, for the boys. And his mother had done her best to help him. But his heart had become cold and hard and unyielding. He lived for his sons and he worked to keep the memories and the grief at bay.

The holidays were so hard without her here.

Then he looked through a window and saw another woman standing in his kitchen. A burnished-blond-haired, green-eyed woman prone to getting herself into sticky situations. That woman had come to his aid without question today.

He watched as she laughed and smiled down at one of the boys. When Sam turned around, Rory heaved a great breath, tears forming in his eyes.

Sam was smiling up at Goldie.

She'd won over his son, just as she'd won over him.

He fell for her right then and there.

Goldie glanced around. She'd heard a car and now she saw Rory's truck out in the driveway. "I think your dad's home," she said to Sam.

The boy's eyes widened. "Are you gonna tell him?"

"Not my place," she said. "I'm leaving that up to you. But I strongly suggest you tell your Dad what you did and why. He'll understand."

Sam didn't look so sure. "Okay," he said, his eyes downcast. But then he glanced up at her and smiled in such a sweet way, Goldie fell for him right then and there.

Was this how it felt to be a mother?

She squelched the tears misting in her eyes.

She'd sent Grams and Carla home so Grams could rest in her own house and take her medicine. The girls were drawing at the dining table and Tyler had awoken from his nap and was playing with his toy trucks by the fire. The house was sparkling clean in spite of four kids messing it up every hour on the hour, and the soup and biscuits were still warming on the stove.

She and Sam had been choosing which pictures to include in the scrapbook. She'd found a folder in his room and put the photos in it to keep them safe. And she'd promised Sam she'd get back with him so he could help her make the keepsake in time for Christmas.

"Now remember, I'll figure out a way to get you out of the house and over to Grams to work on our special project."

"Okay," he said. "Do I have to tell Dad tonight? About the locket?"

Goldie smiled down at him but held firm. "You tell him when you think the time is right. Your dad loves you, Sam. He'll forgive you."

The back door opened then and Rory walked in. "Well, look what a pretty picture—you two busy in the kitchen and everyone else quiet and settled."

Goldie's heart did a little jig of delight. She could get used to seeing him walk through the door every night.

Then she remembered this wasn't her house or her door. And Rory wasn't hers to claim.

But the way he looked at her with a hint of promise in his eyes made her wish for things she couldn't have. She put that wish out of her mind for now.

"How's your mother?"

"Feeling good enough to shoo me and Becky home. Becky's right behind me."

"I sure am," his dark-haired sister said as she rushed through the door. "Oh, Goldie, I can't tell you how much we appreciate this." Becky stopped, glancing around. "What did you do to the house? It looks different."

Tyler ran up to Rory. "We cleaned up. Miss Goldie showed us how to stay organ-nized."

"Organized?" Becky asked, correcting him with a grin. "Well, well." Her girls rushed up to hug her close. "Did you two help?" They bobbed their heads and both started talking at once.

"We had such a good time. Carla helped us make a wreath from nature and we—"

"We helped with the soup and we learned how to label containers and roll socks into neat piles…."

Goldie blocked out all the banter, her eyes focused on Rory. He seemed pleased but he also seemed sad. Was he remembering other homecomings, with Rachel standing here?

Sam had been holding back but now he came around the counter. "Is Grandma gonna get well, Daddy?"

"Yes, she is," Rory said, dropping his jacket on the hall tree bench. "She just has to rest and do some special exercises to get back on track. Her mind's a little fuzzy right now."

Tyler made a face. "Does that hurt?"

"No," Rory said, "not like a stomachache. But it's scary for her. She might have to learn some things all over again."

"Will she miss Christmas?" Tyler asked, tugging at Rory's jeans.

Rory scooped his son up in his arms. "We hope not. But if she's not home, I'll take y'all to see her and give her a present, okay?"

"Okay."

Sam shot Goldie a covert glance. He'd want to have their surprise ready for his grandmother. Goldie smiled at him, conveying her promise with a wink.

After more explanations and reassurances about their grandmother's health, Becky thanked Goldie again and took the girls back to Frances's house.

"Stay here," Rory told Goldie. "I'll get the boys in bed and then we can talk."

She nodded, unable to sit still. Her whole being was humming with awareness. Rory was home and she had to admit it felt so nice imagining being a part of this family.

But do I have the right, Lord?

Goldie didn't know how to handle this sudden rush of feelings. She had too many things to consider. Her job, his children, his mother and about a million other reasons why she should just leave now.

But when Rory came back into the den, his eyes glinting gold in the firelight, Goldie became quiet and still. She couldn't leave him now.

So for once in her tidy, carefully organized life, she didn't try to rearrange things or fix things.

She just stood and stared across the room at the man she was falling in love with.

Chapter Thirteen

"Come and sit," Rory ordered, pointing toward the couch.

Goldie did as he asked, waiting for him to find a spot next to her. "Do you want some dinner?"

He glanced toward the stove. "Maybe later. Right now I just want to sit here in the quiet with you."

"You look tired," she said, acutely aware of the way his gaze flickered over her. "I'm so sorry, Rory. I hope your mother will be better soon."

He let out a long sigh. "Yeah, me, too. I had a lot of time today to think about what might have caused this."

Goldie looked away, toward the fire. She wanted to tell him about Sam thinking it was his fault, but Rory had enough to deal with right now. And she'd promised Sam she wouldn't rat him out to his dad. Her locket was safely hidden underneath her turtleneck sweater for now and that was all that mattered. She'd found it again.

So instead she tried to reassure Rory. "I read about strokes—looked up some information on the Internet. It sounds as if this is very treatable."

"Yes, that's what the doctors say." He leaned forward, his hands clinched together. "I just hope I didn't drive her to this. The boys can be a handful, as you've probably figured out already. But Mom's always a trouper. She helped out right from the beginning." He rubbed a hand across his forehead. "I was pretty messed up the week or so after the funeral. Mom was a rock."

"I can't even begin to understand," Goldie said, the quiet in the room insulating them like a blanket. "It must have been horrible."

"It was." He gazed at the fire, his features shadowed and closed. Then he turned to face her. "I wanted to thank you, Goldie. For what you did today. I don't know why I called you—I shouldn't have. You don't even know my kids that well. But now, I'm glad I did." He took in his surroundings. "Becky was right. The house looks different. Even my two boys seem different. You're the one who made that possible. I'll never forget that."

Goldie didn't know how to respond. Was he hiding his anger that she took over his home, or did he truly appreciate what she'd tried to do for him? He didn't seem angry right now. He appeared sincere and humble, as if he'd actually seen this home for the first time without the veil of grief covering his eyes.

To ease the darkness of her own thoughts, she said, "I was born a neat-freak so it's second nature for me to rearrange and file away and sort things. But I didn't mind. And Grams and Carla enjoyed it, too. We laughed and cleaned, cooked and played games, broke up fights and kissed boo-boos, and even though a mixing bowl got broken and the dog and kids tracked in dirt and leaves, we managed to survive."

"Which one of them broke the bowl?"

"Oh, that would be me, of course. I might be neat but I'm also accident-prone, as you've noticed."

He grinned at that. "Glad it was just a bowl. And I'm glad you're not hurt or stuck in a ditch."

"Me, too." She put a hand to her mouth, stifling a yawn. "Excuse me."

Rory shook his head, smiling. "And you're probably just as tired as I am."

She chuckled. "I think I'll sleep soundly tonight."

He sat back, relaxing against the couch. "Funny how people come into our lives, huh? Of all the couches in the world, I'm glad you passed out on mine."

She looked down at her hands. "Are you sure? I mean, I've been nothing but trouble, don't you think?"

He turned so she could see his face. "I'm beginning to like trouble." Then he glanced around. "Where is that little pile of fur that follows you around?"

"Spike? He went home with Grams and Carla, even though Tyler really wanted him to stay. He loved running around with the kids but I think he's probably snoozing away right now, dreaming of chasing the kids around the yard and hiding in a pile of leaves."

"Are you really going to give him to the boys when you go back to Baton Rouge?"

She nodded, hating to think about leaving Rory and his children and Spike. "I promised." When she looked over at him, she could see the reflection of her own thoughts in his eyes. Did he want her to stay?

Goldie's pulse lifted and skipped at that hope. "I guess I should get home," she said, overwhelmed with a whole passel of new feelings. If she sat here much longer, she might do something really dangerous and tell Rory she didn't want to leave.

"Don't go yet," he pleaded, his gaze saying, "Don't go, ever." Or maybe she was just wishing he'd say that to her.

"Aren't you tired?"

"I was. I am. But I don't want you to go. That soup smells good but I hate eating alone."

She smiled, hoping to ease the pain behind his words. "Then I won't leave just yet."

He took her hand in his. "Are we having a date here?"

She glanced around. "Well, we are alone and I'm not in a crashed car or a drainage canal and I'm conscious and alert."

"Are you seeing two of me?"

"No." One of him was way more than she could handle at this point. "I just see you, Rory. Only you."

"And what do you see, when you look at me?"

The deep intensity of that question threw her and she worked to form her thoughts. "I see a good man who's been through a terrible ordeal. I see a man who loves his children and cares about his family. I see a strong man, determined to take care of everybody." She felt his hand tighten on hers. "And I see a man who also needs to remember to take care of himself."

She watched as he closed his eyes and laid his head back on the puffy couch. Goldie had to fight the urge to reach up and push at the little curls settling across his forehead. Her fingers lifted toward him.

Then he opened his eyes and looked at her. Goldie put her hand down by her side. "I pray every night to do the right thing, for my boys, for my job, for the people I love. But what if that's not enough?"

Goldie wanted to tell him so many things, but she couldn't form the right words. "I think you just have to put one foot in front of the other," she said. "You have to keep moving, Rory. And you need to keep praying." Then she glanced toward the hallway where the boys slept. "But you might want to reach out to the boys a little more. I think Sam needs to talk to you, really talk to you. Or maybe you need to talk to him."

At first, he seemed shocked and angry, a nerve twitching near his mouth as he gritted his teeth. "You picked up on that?"

She nodded, afraid she'd only made him feel worse. "Well, yes. I mean, we both noticed he wasn't exactly thrilled when I entered the picture. But today, I think Sam and I reached a truce of sorts. He's just afraid and confused. And he wants to please you so much. I remember being the same way with my dad."

"Did Sam say something to you today? Something about me?"

Oh boy, did he ever. "We just had a long talk and he kind of warmed up to me. But he blames himself for what happened to your mother."

"Why would he feel that way?"

Realizing she'd let that slip without thinking, Goldie scrambled for words. "I guess because he's the oldest and he thinks he's supposed to be more responsible. I told him it wasn't his fault." To convince him further, she said, "Don't worry. We talked it through and he seems much better now. We're working on a special Christmas gift for you, by the way." Then she put a finger to her lips. "It's a big secret so you have to really act surprised."

Rory turned toward her, his hand still on hers. "I saw him smiling, when I pulled up. I saw you two there through the window and my son was smiling. I don't know what happened between y'all today but I want to thank you again. And you're right. I do need to spend more time with him." Then he touched a finger to her head. "Even after having a concussion, you've still got a pretty good brain inside there, you know."

"And here I thought my head was full of air."

He leaned close, the richness of his golden-brown eyes capturing her in a heady warmth. "Goldie..."

She didn't hear anything else. She just heard him calling her name as he leaned toward her. And then, his lips met hers and she was lost, lost in a longing that caught her breath and made her feel whole again. Rory was kissing her. And she didn't want him to ever stop.

Rory pulled away to stare over at her. "Wow."

Goldie couldn't read the tone of that "Wow." Was it a good kind of wow or an "I've-made-a-huge-mistake-here" wow?

"Is that good or bad?" she finally asked, her words low and shaky.

"Good," he said, his hand on her arm. "And bad."

"Clarify things for me, please."

"It was good, too good." He shifted away. "I don't know how to handle this. Is it too soon? Is there a rule book for a widower kissing another woman?"

Goldie shook her head. "I give advice on getting things in order but I've never had to answer that question, Rory. I guess it all depends on what you feel inside."

He got up to stand with his back to the fire. "Right now, I'm feeling all kinds of things. Guilt and joy, both at the same time. Pain and happiness, all mixed together. I feel like I'm betraying Rachel but I feel like I've just come alive again myself. Is that wrong?"

Goldie stood and headed to the kitchen. "You need to eat."

He followed her, turning her to face him. "Don't go getting all busy on me. We need to talk about this."

"What's there to talk about?" she asked, wishing she could tell him about her feelings. "You're still in love with your wife and that's part of what I like about you. You're the kind of man who stays faithful, Rory. Faithful to God and family and friends. And here I come, messing with all of that. Do you want me to tell you this is wrong? How can I when it feels right to me?"

He let go of her arm. "You've been out there, though. You know more about this kind of thing than I do. I only knew and loved one woman and that woman is gone now. This is all new for me."

"I've had a few relationships, yes, but honestly, I've never dealt with this before, either. None of my ex-boyfriends compare to you—and technically, I haven't even had a date with you yet. How do you explain that?" She turned to the soup on the stove.

"Is *that* a good thing?"

She pulled the foil off the biscuits. "You tell me. Is this good between us? Or are we just asking for trouble? I like you, Rory. But we know what we're up against. I have a fairly good job in Baton Rouge and I'm pushing things with the paper as it is, doing my job long distance and through e-mail. And even though Baton Rouge is not that far away on the map, we're worlds away from each other in our lifestyles. I've been moved from pillar to post most of my life and you're as settled as a cypress tree, roots and all."

"So I'm like an old tree?"

She glanced back to find him smiling at her. "You know what I mean. Besides that, I might have made headway with Sam but your mother wasn't that thrilled about me from what I could tell. And now, you've got a lot more to deal with."

"You mean my mother's stroke?"

"Yes. She's going to need assistance and since you live right here, most of that responsibility will fall on your shoulders."

"I know that and I'm more than willing to take care of her, but that doesn't mean we can't at least continue to get to know each other, does it?"

"But we only have a few days left."

He nodded, his expression solemn as he thought about what she'd said. "We can call and e-mail each other and you'll come now and then to see Ruth, right?"

"Yes, but—"

"Yeah, so, I think we're looking for excuses to fail. Or maybe you're just looking for excuses. Maybe you don't want this because you'd have to deal with my mother and my boys and my life."

"That's not what I'm saying," she protested. But she had to stop and consider that if she decided to let him into her life, she'd have to become a part of his—the way it was and the way it would be. She couldn't ask him to change his life very much. She'd have to be the one doing most of the changing. "I don't know, Rory. I just don't know."

He stared across at her, silent and still. "Then I think that's your answer. Maybe you're *not* ready for this. Maybe you're not ready for me."

Goldie dipped his soup into a bowl and put two biscuits on a plate then poured him a glass of iced tea. "Eat your dinner."

Rory sat down on one of the high stools near the kitchen counter. He pushed the soupspoon around in the chunky beef and vegetables then lifted it to his mouth. After eating a couple of bites, he gazed across at her. "I can't say that I blame you."

Goldie wanted to shout out her fears and her doubts. "What if I'm wrong for you?" she asked. "What if I can't be the woman you think I might be?"

"I can't answer that," he said, taking a biscuit and buttering it. "But I do know this—you've made me smile again. You made Sam smile again. I know this might sound way out there, but I believe God puts certain people in our lives for a reason. And somehow, by the grace of God, you showed up here, Goldie. Here in this house that was sad and gloomy in spite of my best efforts. You've brought something new and bright into our lives. And I can't see anything wrong in that." He chewed his biscuit then said, "And you don't have to be a certain way for me. I kind of like you just the way you are."

"But I'm not Rachel," she explained, getting to the crux of the matter. "I'm not her, Rory."

He dropped the biscuit, his eyes glazing hot. "You

don't have to be. I'd never expect you to be her. No one can replace Rachel. But God has a plan for my life. And maybe you're part of that plan."

"And what about *my* life? Is He up there planning things for me, too? Did He drop me down in this little town for a reason?"

"You came to help your grandmother. Isn't that reason enough?"

She sank back against the counter. "It should be. I love Grams that much. I might get fired, but she needed me."

"Not many people would take that stance."

"We've always helped each other."

"And what about your mother?"

"She's out of the picture."

"Have you talked to her since she left for Europe?"

"Just through e-mail. Phone calls across the Atlantic are expensive."

"You miss her."

"Yes, but why are we talking about my mother?"

"Maybe that's part of God's plan, too."

A fire of frustration burned inside her. "Well, I have a plan, too, Rory. I plan to go back to my safe little world and do my job. I'm good at that one thing, at least."

"You might be good at more than that, Goldie."

"And how am I supposed to figure that out?"

"That's between you and God, I reckon."

She looked down, unsure what to say next. Then she felt the weight of her locket against her skin. When she'd lost it, she thought only bad would come of it.

But now, she had it back and all because a little boy wanted to remember his deceased mother at Christmas. It was a twisted logic but in a strange way, Sam's need to do something special for his mother had brought Goldie and him closer together today. It was as if God had somehow forced both of them together. Or was she just grasping at hope? Rory's mother had a stroke; that certainly couldn't have been part of God's plan.

But it made them stop and think about how things hadn't been going along as well as they'd thought.

Maybe Rory was onto something. Maybe God had been working on both of them and she was just too blind to see that. But how could she be sure?

"You're right. This is between God and me. And I'll have to be the one to figure it out."

Rory pushed his finished soup away then got up. "Well, let me know when you do get things all figured out."

Goldie could tell she'd hurt him. "I'm sorry," she said. "Look, it's late and you've had an awful day. Just get some rest."

He lifted his chin a notch as she walked to the door and gathered her coat and scarf. "Thanks again."

She could tell from his tone that she'd messed up. Was he mad at her because she had cold feet or because she wasn't so sure about the God part of all of this?

"I'll see you later."

"All right." He walked her to the door then pulled

her around. "We can make this right, Goldie. It might take some time but we've got time."

She stared up at him, wishing she could get this all straight and tidy in her mind and in her heart. "Or I could make a mess of things for you, Rory. I don't know if I'm willing to take that risk."

His eyes flashed with fire. "Or maybe you're just not willing to take on the three of us—my boys and me. Maybe we just don't fit in with your perfectly controlled life."

His words hurt her to the core, cutting off her breath and her hope. "You know something, Rory, you really need to get over this notion that you're a burden on everyone around you. Have you ever stopped to think we're all here to help you because we care about you and those children? Or have you just been so wrapped up in misery, you can't even see the suffering of your own son?"

He backed away, shock making him go pale. "You have no reason to say that. You don't know anything about my son."

Goldie swallowed back the painful lump in her throat. "I know enough, Rory."

Then she turned, left his house and hurried to her car. And she didn't dare look back, because if she did, she would return to him and hold him and tell him she was sorry. And she'd tell him that she'd gotten to know Sam really well today.

And that she'd found her locket, too.

Chapter Fourteen

Christmas Eve

Rory stared out the window, taking in the dry leaves and the bare gray trees surrounding his property. He had a beautiful piece of land here, full of cypress and pines, oak and sycamore trees. Just a few weeks ago, these woods had been full of bright oranges and brilliant yellows, the leaves turning with a perfect symmetry almost overnight.

And now, most of the leaves were scattered to the wind. And so was his spiraling and chaotic life.

Because of Goldie.

Fitting, even her name made him think of the changing seasons. He'd lost Rachel in the spring on a perfectly beautiful night where the dogwoods glowed white and ethereal in the surrounding woods. He'd mourned her through Easter and the worst parts of summer. He'd lost her through someone else's brutality and now that person was serving a life sentence in prison. But in some ways, Rory was serving that same sentence, too.

If I'd only been able to go to the store for her that night, he thought over and over again. If only. He'd asked God to give him answers but he knew he'd find the answers in heaven. But right now, he was still here on earth. And he was falling in love with a woman who was completely different from his wife. A woman who was afraid to lose control and let him love her.

Lord, is it possible to love two women at the same time?

Rory had never felt so torn in his life. Since work had been kind of slow due to the winter season, he was at odds all the way around. He'd raked leaves with the boys, trying to bring Sam out of his own mourning. He'd even taken them with him on a quick run to get a doe out of a mud pit, just to have them near. Christmas was hard on all of them but this year with his mom sick, it would be especially hard. Frances always fussed and cooked and spoiled them. Rory knew he'd failed his boys in the most important way. He'd neglected to actually talk to them about their mother.

Goldie had been right on that account, but he'd been too angry and hurt to tell her so.

I'm trying, Lord, he said on a fervent prayer. *I'm trying. I'll give up Goldie if it will bring me closer to my boys. It's the only thing I can do. It's the right thing to do.*

"And I'm that kind of man," he said to himself, his tone sarcastic and bitter.

Maybe if he concentrated on keeping busy, he could find a way to work through all these strange feelings. He wanted Goldie in his life but he wasn't sure he was ready to accept that he was in love with her. And she sure wasn't ready to accept that, either. So instead of standing here brooding on it, he made a list and set out to cook Christmas dinner tomorrow for his sons and his mother.

Becky would bring her family over after Christmas to spend some time with their mother but right now, it was up to Rory to make things special. Frances had improved enough to come home, on the condition that she'd rest and let everyone else spoil her for a change. Rory thought that was a good idea.

When he heard a car in the drive, he opened the back door and waved at the friend who'd taken the boys along with her children to see the live nativity village set up behind the church. The boys rushed in, throwing hats and jackets here and there, excited about petting a real donkey and two baby lambs.

"Mrs. Evans said you helped find the animals for the nativity scene, Dad," Tyler exclaimed, clearly impressed.

Sam chimed in. "I told my friends you know a lot about animals." His eyes shone bright with pride.

Rory let out a held breath. Maybe his older son was

slowly healing in his own way. The minister and the church counselors had told Rory that children were more resilient than adults when it came to grief. He hoped that was true. But he couldn't forget that Goldie had helped Sam, too.

Even if she wasn't speaking to Rory, she'd kept her pledge to Sam to help him with his big surprise. She'd picked up Sam the other night, waiting in the car for him to come out. Rory had waved to her and she'd just smiled and waved back, her eyes devoid of any joy.

Putting that image away for now, he said, "Hey, I have an idea and I need y'all to help me. I want to cook Christmas dinner for Grandma and bring it to her tomorrow. What do you think?"

"Can she get out of bed?" Sam asked, swiping a hand across his red nose.

Rory nodded. "She's okay physically. She just has some memory and coordination problems. But she's doing fine and she's already started her therapy sessions. Her friend took her to the first one yesterday. But we'll go there and cook so she won't have to lift a finger."

"What's a cordon-nation problem, Daddy?" Tyler inquired.

"It means she might have trouble remembering how to spell and read. Her thoughts get all mixed up so she has to learn some things over again."

"I can help her read," Tyler offered. "I can read pretty good."

"I know you can," Rory replied, smiling. The boys

had become very protective of their grandmother since Frances had come home yesterday. And Becky was staying through the New Year so Rory could get a break.

"Who's with Grandma now?" Sam posed the question as he nabbed a cookie from the jar on the counter.

"She has a day nurse," Rory explained. "We thought that would be a good idea since I had to finish up some work today. And she has friends coming over tonight to visit, since she can't go to the Christmas Eve service at church. We'll visit her later, too. But tomorrow we can give the nurse a rest. Right now we need to make this list and buy groceries." He grabbed a pen and a notepad.

Tyler shrugged. "I wish she hadn't got sick."

"Me, either, buddy, but sometimes things like this happen."

"Like when Mom died?" Sam guessed, his eyes going dark again.

Rory almost went back to his old standard way of brushing off hard questions. But instead of repeating that things just happened and changing the subject, he clarified, "Yes, son. Like that. It hurts a lot but we have to keep on keeping on." He ruffled Sam's hair. "Your mom would want us to do that. She'd want us to have a good Christmas and she'd tell us that we're blessed because we have each other."

Tyler looked up at Rory. "Is Miss Goldie coming over for Christmas?"

"Maybe," Rory replied. He wanted to see her on Christmas day. He had her gift. "I hope we get to see her again before she goes back to Baton Rouge."

"She's supposed to bring Spike, remember?" Tyler said, his expression hopeful.

"I remember, son."

Sam glanced around then back to Rory. "Daddy, I…I need to tell you something."

"What?" Rory asked, dread building up inside him. Did Sam want to talk some more about his mother's death?

Sam gave his little brother another glance. "Not right now, though."

Rory took that as a hint. "Hey, Tyler, why don't you go and wash your hands for lunch. I'll call you when it's ready."

Tyler shrugged again. "I can't see any dirt on my hands, but whatever." He took off running toward the bathroom.

Rory had to smile at that. Tyler sounded like an echo of his older brother. When he turned back to Sam, the boy looked so dejected Rory touched him on the shoulder. "You know you can talk to me about anything don't you, son?"

Sam nodded, his head down.

Rory took him over to the couch. "Let's talk, then."

Sam let out a long sigh, his hands in his lap. "I did something bad."

Surprised at that solemn admission, Rory playfully

pushed at Sam's shirtsleeve. "Like what? Did you get in another fight with your brother over the game remote?"

Sam shook his head. "Worse than that."

"Okay, so you forgot to pick up your dirty clothes again."

Sam didn't respond. He sat staring at his hands.

"Just tell me now, Sam. Let's get it out in the open."

Sam finally looked up at him, the expression on his face mirroring the doubt and fear in his eyes. "I…I found Miss Goldie's locket."

Rory let out a chuckle and a big sigh. "You did? Well, that's nothing to be so sad about. Where'd you find it? Where is it now? We need to let her know right away."

Sam shook his head. "She knows already."

That cut the chuckle right out of Rory's throat. "What?" He realized Sam had seen her this week. He must have given her the locket then.

But Sam's frown was full of despair not pride. "I told her about it the other day when she was here with her friend and her grandma."

"You did?" Wondering why Goldie hadn't mentioned it, he stared at his son. They must have found it when they were out playing in the leaves and maybe Goldie just forgot to tell him. "Why didn't y'all tell me?"

Sam fell back against the couch, his chin jutting out. "Miss Goldie said I had to be the one. She said it wasn't her place."

Rory put two fingers to his nose, pinching the throbbing pain developing there. “Okay, let’s start from the beginning, Sam. Tell me what happened with the locket.”

Sam looked at the Christmas tree. “I found it the night Miss Goldie had her wreck.”

A great weight settled like an anchor in Rory’s stomach. “That was about three weeks ago. And you knew we were searching for it. Are you telling me you had it the whole time and didn’t say anything?”

“Yes, sir.”

Now he could at least see why Goldie hadn’t brought up the locket the last time he’d seen her. And he suddenly understood very well that she indeed knew more about his son than he did. She’d been protecting Sam.

Rory looked at his son, wondering what else he didn’t know. “Sam, you heard how much that necklace meant to Goldie and you saw me looking for it everywhere around here. Why did you feel the need to hide the locket, son?”

Sam finally glanced up, his eyes brimming with fear and doubt. “I thought I’d put it on Mama’s grave. It was so pretty and…I wanted to just put it on her grave but I was afraid you’d get mad at me. So I…hid it.”

Rory bit his lip, his own emotions swelling until he thought he’d burst. He had to repeat the whole thing just to make sense of it. “So even though you knew it was wrong to hide the locket, you kept it because you wanted to put it on Mommy's grave?"

"Yes, sir."

"But, Sam, even though that was a thoughtful thing to do for your mother, you know that was wrong, don't you?"

"Yes, sir. Miss Goldie told me that was sweet but since the locket didn't belong to me, it was better to give it back to her. She said Mom wouldn't want stolen jewelry on her grave."

Rory listened to his son's words, trying to piece this puzzle together. "And Miss Goldie promised not to tell me, right?"

Sam bobbed his head. "She said I had to tell you and that you loved me so you'd forgive me. Is that true?"

Rory's heart hammered an erratic cadence deep inside his chest. "Yes, of course that's true," he assured him, reaching over to Sam. "I love you." He held his son close, feeling the tension radiating from the little boy's body. "But you understand that what you did was wrong?"

"Yes, sir."

Rory closed his eyes, remembering his harsh words to Goldie. "What made you decide to give it back to Goldie?"

Sam pulled away, his eyes full of moisture. "'Cause MeeMaw found it in one of the Christmas bags and when she asked me about it, I told her I'd put it there and she got really upset and then—"

"And then she got sick, right?"

Sam nodded again, tears falling down his face. "I didn't mean to make her mad or get her all sick. I just hid it there until I could take it to Mama. I wasn't trying to be mean, honest, Dad. I just wanted Mama to have it. I didn't want Miss Goldie around. I wanted Mama."

Rory gritted his teeth against the tears pricking at his own eyes as he pulled his son back into his arms. "I know, son. I know." He kissed Sam's dark curls. "I miss her, too. And while putting the locket on her grave would have been a nice gesture, you were wrong to hide it. You understand that now. And you did the right thing, telling me the truth, okay?"

Sam's muffled reply sent ripples of love and shame throughout Rory's system. He'd failed his son. He should have talked to Sam more about Rachel, about her death and everything that had held them apart since then. But he'd been so busy trying to be normal, trying to put one foot in front of the other like everyone had told him to do, that he hadn't noticed his son's suffering.

Well, Goldie had noticed and instead of getting angry and berating Sam for literally stealing something that was very precious to her, she'd turned things around and forced the issue by befriending Sam and convincing him to tell his father the truth.

How did he thank her for that? For giving his son back to him, for showing him that his heart wasn't completely broken after all? How could he ever convince her that she belonged in his life? Goldie would make a wonderful mother to his children. He could see that so clearly now. Somehow he had to convince her of that.

Wiping at his own eyes, he held Sam by the shoulders. "So Miss Goldie has her locket?"

Sam nodded. "She put it on after I gave it to her. She was really glad to have it back." He looked up at Rory, a new light shining in his eyes. "And you know what, Dad? I felt better, telling her the truth."

"I'm sure you did. I'm so proud of you. Your mom would be proud, too."

"That's what Miss Goldie said."

"And you two, are things better between you now?"

Another bob of the head. "She's helping me..." Sam stopped, his mouth dropping open. "Never mind. It's a surprise."

"A good surprise?"

"Uh-huh."

"Then I can live with that." Rory reached out a hand to Sam. Sam offered his own and Rory shook it, man to man. "I *am* proud of you, son. You confessed to something you did and you told me why you did it. You and I both are blessed because your mother was a wonderful woman and she'd be so touched that you wanted to put something nice on her grave. She knows you did the right thing and you need to remember that."

Sam blinked then sniffed. "Will God forgive me, too?"

"Of course He will," Rory confirmed. "God always gives us a second chance to make things right."

Sam's expression lifted and changed right in front of Rory's eyes, his frown relaxing into a soft smile. "I like Miss Goldie. I didn't at first, but I do now. I'm sorry I hid the locket."

"Well, it's all over now," Rory said. "And, Sam, you didn't cause MeeMaw to get sick. She was already ill, so unhealthy that something went wrong inside her brain. But she's going to be better soon. I promise you, this is not your fault."

Sam lowered his gaze again. "Miss Goldie told me that it's not anybody's fault. Does that mean what happened to Mom isn't your fault, then?"

That one hit Rory right in the heart. "I guess it does. But why… How do you know that I blame myself?"

"You said it," Sam replied. "I heard you telling MeeMaw that one day when you were sad. I heard you and so I thought…I thought that if we do bad things, then something bad happens to people because of us. You told MeeMaw that if you hadn't been late, you could have gone to the store for Mama and she'd still be alive."

Rory listened to the heartfelt words coming out of his son's mouth and silently prayed to God to take this burden from his son. And him. "I shouldn't have said that, Sam. I was just confused and I missed your mama."

"Miss Goldie said you still love Mom. Do you?"

"Of course I do. I'll always love your mom. And I do wish I could have been the one who went to the store that night but I have to stop blaming myself, don't I?"

Sam nodded. "I don't blame you. I don't blame anybody."

Rory ruffled his son's curls. "I'm glad to hear that. I think it's time you and I both stop punishing ourselves for things we can't control, okay?"

"Okay." Sam settled back again. "I hope Miss Goldie comes on Christmas. Then we can give you the present I made. And we get to see Spike again."

"I hope so, too, son," Rory said, nodding. "In fact, I'm going by there on my way to get groceries and invite her and Miss Ruth for dinner. What do you think about that?"

"That's okay with me," Sam replied, the relief on his face evident.

But it was a heartbreaking relief for Rory. How long had his son carried this burden, wondering if his own father was the blame for his mother's death, wondering how to love a man who couldn't forgive himself?

Rory thought about Christ dying on the cross and remembered the burden had already been lifted, from his shoulders and from his son's, too. Because of another son long ago who'd been willing to keep the burden of sins on His back. So men such as Rory could sit here by the fire and hug their own children close, knowing they were forgiven.

It was sobering and humbling and Rory thanked God he'd finally seen the truth there in Sam's eyes.

And he wanted to thank Goldie, for rescuing him from his own doubts and despair. He sent out a prayer that she'd forgive him for being so pigheaded and for pushing her so hard. Loneliness and confusion had clouded his vision.

His head was clear now. And he wanted her in his life.

"Are you gonna go see her?" Sam asked, tugging at Rory's sleeve.

"I am. But I can't leave you and Tyler here by yourselves. I guess y'all will have to go to the store with me. And to see Miss Goldie, too."

Sam got up, a new energy radiating around him. "I'll go tell Tyler." Then he turned around. "We never had lunch, Dad."

"No, we didn't," Rory said. "How about we see if Goldie wants to go for pizza with us *before* we buy groceries?"

"Okay."

And with that, his son ran down the hallway to get his brother. While Rory sat staring at the twinkling star on the Christmas tree.

Chapter Fifteen

Goldie pulled her grandmother's car up to the curb at the Baton Rouge Metropolitan Airport, her hands clammy on the wheel. Was she crazy to be here? It was Christmas Eve, after all. Glancing around, she wondered for the hundredth time if she'd made the right decision.

"Well, I'm here now." Goldie got out of the car and looked around. A crowd of holiday travelers rushed by, suitcase wheels grinding on the hard, cold concrete.

She pulled her leather jacket close then checked her watch. She was on time. She only hoped the flight would be.

And suddenly, she saw her mother coming through the terminal at a fast pace, tugging her bright purple suitcase behind her. Angela was wearing all black and carrying a shiny patent black-and-white-patterned tote to match.

Goldie braced herself. She still couldn't get over the shock of her mother's phone call from the Atlanta airport early this morning.

"I'm coming home, honey. Pick me up in Baton Rouge at two o'clock. Don't be late."

And just like that, Goldie's world had gone into a tailspin. Her wayward mother had decided to surprise them with a Christmas Eve visit. On the one hand, Goldie thanked God for this gift of a second chance. On the other hand, Goldie wished she could run, get on one of those planes and fly away from her troubles.

But no, that's what her mother did. Goldie always stayed behind and kept things organized. Goldie always put everything in its rightful place, even her love life.

Grinding her teeth against the cold, she took a deep breath. She'd organized her grandmother's house and Rory's house, and managed to keep her work organized and never missed a deadline. She'd answered Buried in Bossier with a new insight and she'd dashed off a holiday organization tip sheet that her editor at the paper was raving about. In fact, she was so efficient she always got through the worst of circumstances, like losing the man she loved, with noble aplomb.

This week, she'd helped Sam make two small scrapbooks, rearranged her grandmother's pantry yet again and bought colorful storage bins for all the Christmas decorations that she would take down before she left for the city and her own tidy little apartment.

But what was she supposed to do with her mother?

"Hi, Mom," Goldie called, pasting a smile on her face when her mother emerged onto the sidewalk. "I'm here."

"Why, you sure are. I knew you'd be right on time. You just don't have it in you to be late, do you, suga'?"

"And it's great to see you, too, Mom."

Angela tossed her own wavy burnished-brown hair and laughed. "Hello, darlin'." She hugged Goldie close. "You're so thin."

"And you're so blunt."

Goldie put her mother's suitcase in the trunk then got in the car. Angela tossed her tote in the back. "What on earth are you doing driving this old gas-guzzler?"

"My car's in the shop."

Angela pulled down the sun visor, saw there wasn't a mirror and frowned. Snapping it back up, she turned to Goldie. "Why? What's wrong with it?"

"Oh, major damage to the front bumper, the hood and some missing parts that fell out when I hit a tree."

"You hit a tree? How on earth did that happen?"

"The roads were icy."

Angela gave her daughter a long, glaring look. "Ice? In Louisiana? Honey, are you sure you're feeling okay?"

"We had a big ice storm about three weeks ago and yes, I'm sure. I hit a bad spot and, well, I wrecked my car. But I'm okay. Just got a knot on my already-hard head."

And fell in love with a not-so-perfect family.

Her mother's blue-green eyes slanted like a cat's as she studied Goldie's head to make sure she was all right. "I guess I've missed a lot."

"Why'd you come home so soon, anyway?" Goldie asked, trying to be patient, trying to be thankful.

Angela waved a hand in the air. "Well, honey, there I was standing looking up at the Eiffel Tower. It was beautiful. You know, Paris is the City of Lights."

"Yes, I've heard that."

"Well, I got this awful feeling. I got homesick. I wanted to see the Christmas lights in Natchitoches and the cute little lights in Viola and I wanted to drive up to Shreveport and do the whole Trail of Lights from Shreveport and Bossier City all the way over into Jefferson and Marshall in Texas."

Goldie nodded, pretending to understand. "And so…"

"And so, I booked a flight home. And just in time for Christmas. And wait until you see what I brought you."

"Mom, I've never known you to be homesick."

"I know. It floored me, too. But, honey, I'm getting old and ornery, and I just want my own bed, my frayed pajamas and I don't want to see another tour bus for a long time."

Goldie smiled over at her mother. "I'm glad you're home, Mom."

Angela patted her hand. "And besides, your grandmother sent me an urgent text message. Something about a man named Rory putting you all in a tizzy."

Goldie almost lost control of the car. "Grams knows how to text?"

"Yep. Pretty good at it, too. I had to ask a teenager on the tour what she was saying. Who knew 'RUP' means 'read up please' and 'WAY' means 'where are you?' When I didn't answer at first, I got another one saying '4COL,GTHM AEAP.'

"What does that mean?" Goldie asked, sick at her stomach. She texted a lot herself but even she didn't know all the shorthand.

"For crying out loud, get home as early as possible," Angela explained with a shrug.

Since she was stopped at a red light, Goldie gently banged her head against the ancient steering wheel. "I can't believe this."

"Well, aren't you glad to see me?"

"Yes," Goldie replied, too stunned to say anything else.

"Now before we get back to your grandmother's house, let's stop in Lafayette, have a nice cup of Louisiana coffee and talk about this Rory. And I want to hear everything." She winked. "After all, isn't that what a mother is for?"

Rory pulled up to Ruth's house with high expectations and sweaty palms. He'd gone to the grocery store first so he wouldn't have to rush this. So he and the boys had spent two hours in the crowded place, making sure they had all the ingredients for a passable meal. He'd finally fed the boys in the snack bar, promising them a nice meal later, hopefully with Goldie.

"I don't see Miss Ruth's car, Dad," Sam said.

"Neither do I," Rory replied. "Let's just go check since we're here."

They all piled out of the truck. Rory could hear Spike barking inside the house. That was a good sign at least.

But the woman who opened the door wasn't Goldie. Or Miss Ruth.

"Uh, hi," Rory said. "Is Goldie here?"

The woman gave him a once-over look that might have served for sizing up a rodent. "No and your knock probably woke up her grandmother."

"I'm sorry," Rory apologized, lowering his voice. "I just wanted to talk to Goldie."

"Well, you can't," the woman declared. "I'm Phyllis, Ruth's friend. Goldie called me to come and stay with her. Goldie went to Baton Rouge."

With that, the woman slammed the door in his face.

"She wasn't very nice," Tyler said, looking down at his sneakers.

But Rory didn't care about the woman's rudeness. He only cared that Goldie had left. On Christmas Eve. Without saying goodbye.

"She didn't bring Spike to us," Sam said, his chin jutting out. "And she promised." He stared at the door. "And what about— Never mind."

Rory knew what his son was thinking. She hadn't even bothered to make sure Sam got the presents he'd made for Rory and Frances.

"How could she just leave like that, Dad?" Sam asked.

Rory hated the disappointment in his son's question. But he felt that same disappointment inside his heart.

"I don't know, son. Maybe she had an emergency."

"Yeah, right." Sam was back to his old cynical self.

And Rory couldn't blame the boy. A crushing weight settled on his chest as he guided his boys back to the truck. Goldie had bolted; she'd run away without even giving them a chance. Or maybe she'd left because he hadn't really given her a chance.

Goldie pulled into the driveway, a great exhaustion weighing her down. She'd poured out her heart to her mother, something she wasn't used to doing.

But even after tears and ranting and hoping and discussing, and even though she was drained, she'd appreciated having her mother to talk to. And to sagely tell her, "Go find the man and tell him you love him, honey. The rest will all just have to work itself out."

What a Christmas this was turning out to be.

They walked in to find Phyllis fussing as she wiped at the tile floor in the kitchen. "That dog of yours had an accident."

"I'm so sorry," Goldie said, mortified. Phyllis was a dear friend to her grandmother but she wasn't the most pleasant person in the world. "Let me finish cleaning that."

Phyllis lifted up with a groan, her bright red sweat suit reminding Goldie of Mrs. Claus. "Where's Grams?"

"She's just getting up from her nap," Phyllis said, already gathering her things. "But for the life of me, I don't know how she got any rest. Dogs barking, people knocking at the door—"

"Who stopped by?"

"Oh, a man and two boys. I think I've seen him at church. Young, nice-looking but kind of dense. I told him you'd gone to Baton Rouge and he just stood there with his mouth open."

Goldie looked at her stunned mother. "Rory."

"Rory," Phyllis echoed with a triumphant smile. "I knew him. Just couldn't remember his name."

"Rory was here?"

Phyllis stared across the room at Goldie. "Yes, that's what I said. Now you're looking daft, just like he did."

"That's because she's in love with him," Angela asserted, impatience fueling her declaration. "Phyllis, why don't you stay awhile. I'll go get Mama Ruth up and give her a big old hug, and we'll make a pot of coffee and I'll get out the goodies I brought for y'all."

"You brought me something?" Phyllis asked, looking dumbfounded.

"I sure did," Angela replied. Then she grinned. "Now who's looking daft?"

Phyllis waved a hand in the air. "Good to have you back in town, Angela."

"Good to be back." Angela looked at Goldie. "Go while you can, honey. And don't look back."

Goldie grabbed Spike and did as her mother told her. For once.

She pulled up to the house and sat in the car, an anxious Spike right beside her, watching as the man and the two little boys laughed and talked inside the kitchen. Across the big, open room, the Christmas tree sparkled with hundreds of tiny blinking lights. The wreath on the French door glistened from the tall security light out in the backyard and up over the trees, a bright star shined as a beacon to the world.

A beacon to all of those who had lost hope.

"You know something, Spike? I've come full circle."

The little dog hopped from his spot on the old blanket into her lap, waiting for her to finish. "This all started when I saw my boyfriend holding a little puppy—and another woman. That scene, as awful as it was, brought me to this scene, and you." She stroked the little dog then hugged him close. "I like this scene better."

Goldie got out, determined to get this relationship organized. Spike barked his excitement and three dark-haired heads came up. Then she heard footsteps and watched as the boys rushed to open the door.

"Spike!" Tyler ran out, reaching up to the little dog. "You came back."

Goldie giggled and handed Spike over to Tyler. "Of course he came back. I promised, didn't I?"

Sam stood to the side. "That woman told us you'd left."

Goldie glanced from Sam's hopeful face to Rory's surprised one. "Well, that woman didn't have the Christmas spirit and so she didn't take the time to explain things. I didn't go back to Baton Rouge for good. I just went to pick up my mother at the airport. She came home for Christmas."

Rory's eyes met hers, a faint smile replacing his frown. "That's good, isn't it?"

"It is good," Goldie said. "And I'm sorry y'all thought I'd left you. I'd never leave without saying goodbye and giving you Spike."

Sam nudged her. "What about…?"

"Right here." Goldie patted her big bag. "May we come in?"

"Sure," Rory agreed, grinning now. "You're just in time. We visited my mom and then we ordered pizza."

"How is she?"

"She's doing pretty good. Glad to be home. My aunt came up from New Orleans to spend the night with her and we'll all be there tomorrow. I'm going to cook."

"Wow. That sounds like fun."

He shut the door then glanced to where the boys were playing with Spike. "Goldie, I—"

Sam came running up. "I told him, Miss Goldie. About the locket."

"Yes, he did," Rory said. "And we're both sorry for what we put you through."

Goldie smiled down at Sam then pulled out her necklace from under her blouse. "It's over now and I have my locket back. And I think Grams was right. It did bring me good, but it's not so much about the jewelry. It's about finding the good in my own life—God's blessings and His plan for me."

Rory's gaze washed over her, understanding coloring his eyes in a rich gold that rivaled the lights on the tree. "Can you stay awhile?"

"I sure can." She leaned down to Sam. "After supper, we'll give your dad his gift, okay?"

Sam nodded. "I'll get out the paper plates."

They ate and laughed and chatted. Goldie told them all about her mother and how Grams had texted her.

"She called in reinforcements?" Rory asked.

"I guess so. I can't believe Grams knew how to text anyone and that my mother came all that way for me."

"I can," he replied. "We need to talk."

"Not before presents," Tyler declared. "You promised we could open one tonight, remember?"

"I do."

"It's okay," Goldie said. "I can stay awhile."

They went over by the tree and Tyler opened a remote-control car. He went off to try it out in the hallway. Sam opened his—an LSU jacket. Then he looked at Goldie. "Now?"

"Now," she repeated, reaching into her bag. She handed the two boxes to Sam. "The green one's your grandmother's. And the red one is your dad's."

Sam put the green one under the tree then sheepishly handed the other one to Rory. "For you, from me."

"Thanks, Sam." Rory quickly opened the box then lifted out the scrapbook inside. Goldie watched, holding her breath. Sam came to sit by her, reaching out for her hand.

The look on Rory's face as he studied the pages made her fall in love with him all over again. His eyes went dark and then turned bright and moist. He moved his fingers over the photographs of his family, his eyes scanning the words written there in Sam's broad handwriting.

"I remembered some of it and Miss Goldie helped me with the other stuff."

Rory looked up, his fingers moving over a wedding picture, a baby picture of each boy, a T-ball game, Sam at bat, a beach vacation and a family Christmas picture taken at church. After seeing several more pictures, he swallowed and tried to speak, then swallowed again. "This is the best gift I've ever been given, Sam. This means the world to me and so do you and your brother. Thank you."

Sam beamed with pride. "We made MeeMaw one,

too. With pictures of Grandpa and Mom and you and Aunt Becky and the girls and us. And we have a picture to put on Mom's grave."

"I know MeeMaw will love hers, and so will your mom." Rory reached out, his arms opening for Sam. "I love you, son."

Sam rushed into his daddy's arms while Goldie discreetly wiped at her eyes. While she watched them, she held her locket and thanked God for leading her to this family.

An hour later, Rory came up the hallway from tucking in the boys and Spike and found his kitchen clean and his living room tidy.

"You've been busy."

"Sorry. Habit."

"It's a nice habit." He stared at her, sitting there on the couch where he'd found her. She was so still. Goldie rarely sat still. "So…"

"So," she said. "Here we are."

"You came back."

"I did."

"But you're leaving again, right?"

"That depends." She leaned forward, her gaze holding Rory's. "We could take things slow, see where it goes, okay? That is, if you're still interested in that kind of arrangement."

He grinned at her nervousness and her formality. "I think I can live with that. I'm not in a big rush."

"Me, either."

Rory fell down on the couch. "Who am I kidding? I'm in a really big rush." Then he kissed her, showing her the urgency of that rush.

"Wow," she said when he let her go.

"Is that a good wow?"

"Yes, very good. Taking things slow is highly overrated anyway. And you kissed me again."

He reached for her hand. "Yes and I know what kissing you did to me the first time. It threw me. But in a good way."

"Glad we clarified that." She pulled away, her hand touching her necklace. "It sure threw me, too."

Rory took one of her hands back in his. "I'm sorry about how I treated you the other night."

"I'm sorry I couldn't tell you the truth about my locket."

He kissed her again. "You promised Sam. And you were right. He and I had a good long talk and things are better, so much better. So there. All is forgiven."

Her smile became radiant. "Yes, all is forgiven."

"I still owe you a real date."

"I'll hold you to that."

He gave her a quick peck on the cheek. "So, will you bring your mother and grandmother to Christmas dinner?"

"Are you sure? Won't that be a lot on your mother?"

"She wants you both there and I won't let her get too tired. Besides, she said you're practically family now."

"She did? When did she say that?"

"Today, when I told her I loved you and somehow, I was going to make you mine."

"You told her that?"

"I did. I do—love you." Then he jumped up. "I forgot. I have your present."

Her green eyes sparkled right along with the tree lights. She carefully opened the tiny box then lifted the lid. "Oh, Rory."

"It's a locket," he said, grinning. "To replace the one I'd thought you'd lost."

Goldie rubbed her fingers over the round gold medallion then opened it. "It's beautiful. I'll have to get a picture to put in here."

"But you found *your* locket."

She pulled him down beside her and hugged him tight.

"Yes, I certainly did." She kissed him then put her hand on her heart. "And I think it's right here. I guess I just had to find a way to open it."

Rory pulled her hand up to his lips, kissing her fingers. "So, I know the way to Baton Rouge."

"That's good. And I know the way home."

Rory's heart opened and filled with hope. He stared down at the little picture book on the table, knowing he'd make new memories with Goldie. "I love you, but I think I already told you that."

"I love you, too."

"You owe me a new couch pillow."

"It's in the car. Grams helped me make it." She got up. "I'll go and get it."

But Rory pulled her back. "Oh, no. You might fall into a hole and I'd have to come dig you out."

"Good point. But you'll like the pillow. It says 'Home, sweet home' on one side and 'Go, LSU' on the other."

He tugged her to the fire so they could hug each other close while they looked at the Christmas tree.

"Don't leave me, Goldilocks."

"I won't," she promised. "I went about it all the wrong way, but at last I've found the right man."

He laughed then kissed the top of her head. "Think you can handle me and the boys?"

"I think so." She leaned up, her gaze holding his. "In fact, I think this family is just right for me. A perfect fit."

"Merry Christmas," Rory said.

"Merry Christmas yourself."

They stood there for a long time, holding each other as they looked beyond the tree, out the window and up into the night sky, their hopes pinned on the star guiding them toward the perfect gift of God's grace and love.

Finally, Rory whispered, "Hey, you know anything about putting a bike together?"

Goldie grinned. "No, but I'm willing to learn. And I can organize all the parts for you."

"Let's get started, then," Rory replied, his hand in hers.

And from the smile on her face, he knew Goldie was finally ready to do just that.

* * * * *

Dear Reader,

We all love gifts. My friends know that I love receiving presents. But it took me a long time to realize in my case, it's not so much the presents I receive but rather the gift of friendship and love that comes with the presents. In this case, Goldie and Rory were both searching for the kind of gift that would bring them love and friendship. Rory had lost his wife so his heart was sad and bitter. Goldie had a cynical nature that didn't leave much room for God's love. But together, they managed to figure things out—with the help of Rory's family and Goldie's grandmother Ruth.

This is the kind of perfect gift we all crave—unconditional love and a strong family connection. Sometimes, things go wrong in relationships. We might lose a loved one to death or we might find ourselves cast off by a relative or a friend who can't forgive us for something from the past. But if we turn to God, He can give us that unconditional love that does not change like a shifting shadow. God's love is the one perfect gift that never wavers. And sometimes, in finding His gift, we can overcome all obstacles and find love again. I hope this story brings you a bit of hope and that wherever you are in your relationship with God, you will know that He can offer the best gift of all—His presence in your heart.

Until next time, may the angels watch over you—always.

Lenora Worth

QUESTIONS FOR DISCUSSION

1. What do you consider to be the perfect gift?
2. Have you ever thought about what gifts you have that can help you in your faith?
3. Why do you think Goldie was always organizing things? Do you think she used that as an excuse to get close to people?
4. Do you think clutter tends to make our emotions worse? How can cleaning up your home also help you to clean up your life?
5. Why did Rory fight against loving Goldie? Do you know someone who has lost a loved one? How did that change this person?
6. Sam was suffering because of the trauma of his mother's death. Do you think his acting out stemmed from that loss?
7. Do you know children such as Sam who act out because they can't express what's inside their hearts?
8. Why do you think Rory's mother, Frances, was so afraid of Rory falling for Goldie?

9. Do you think it would be hard to step in where another woman has lived and loved the way Goldie had to do with Rory and his boys?

10. It's hard to be a widower at a young age. Have you ever known someone who lost their spouse in this way?

11. Do you think Rory was wise to follow his heart with Goldie? Have you ever wanted to follow your heart but were afraid you'd be doing the wrong thing?

12. How did their faith finally bring Goldie and Rory to each other?

13. Do you think Goldie will continue to organize things? Do you think this part of her personality will continue but in a better way?

When a young Roman woman is wrenched from the safety of her family and sold into slavery, she finds herself at the mercy of the most famous gladiator in Rome. In God's plan, a master and his slave just might fall in love....

Turn the page for a sneak preview of
THE GLADIATOR
by Carla Capshaw.
Available in November 2009
from Love Inspired® Historical.

Rome, 81 A.D.

Angry, unfamiliar voices penetrated Pelonia's awareness. Floating between wakefulness and dark, she couldn't budge. Every muscle ached. A sharp pain drummed against her skull.

The voices died away, then a woman's words broke through the haze.

"My name is Lucia. Can you hear me?" The woman pressed a cup of water to Pelonia's cracked lips. "What shall I call you?"

Pelonia coughed as the cool liquid trickled down her arid throat. "Pel...Pelonia."

"Do you remember what happened to you? You were struck on the head and injured. I've been giving you opium to soothe you, but you're far from recovered."

Her eyelids too heavy to open, Pelonia licked her chapped lips.

Gradually her mind began to make sense of her surroundings. The warmth must be sunshine, because the scent of wood smoke hung in the air. Her pallet was a coarse woolen blanket on the hard ground. Dirt clung to her skin and each of her sore muscles longed for the softness of her bed at home.

Home.

Where was she if not in the comfort of her father's Umbrian villa? Who was this woman Lucia? She couldn't remember.

Icy fingers of fear gripped her heart as one by one her memories returned. First the attack, then her father's murder. Raw grief squeezed her chest.

Confusion surrounded her. Where was her uncle? She remembered the slave caravan, his threat to sell her, but nothing more.

Panic forced her eyes open. She managed to focus on the young woman's face above her.

"The master will be here soon." A smile tilted Lucia's thin lips, but didn't touch her honey-brown eyes.

"Where…am I?" she asked, the words grating in her throat.

"You're in the home of Caros Viriathos."

The name meant nothing to Pelonia. She prayed God had delivered her into the hands of a kind man, someone who would help her contact her cousin Tiberia.

Her eyes closed with fatigue. "How…how long have I…been here?"

"Four days and this morning. You've been in and out of sleep. I'll order you a bowl of broth. You should eat to bolster your strength."

Four days, and she remembered nothing. Tiberia must be frantic wondering why she'd failed to attend her wedding.

She opened her eyes. "I must—"

"Don't speak. Now that you've woken, Gaius, our master's steward, says you have one week to recover. Then your labor begins."

"My cousin. I must…"

"You're a slave in the Ludus Maximus now. A possession of the *lanista,* Caros Viriathos."

Lanista? A vile *gladiator* trainer?

"No!"

Lucia crossed her arms over her buxom chest. "We will see."

Heavy footsteps crunched on the rushes strewn across the floor. The new arrival stopped out of Pelonia's view.

The nauseating ache in her head increased without mercy. What had she done to make God despise her?

Focusing on Lucia, she saw the young woman's face light with pleasure.

"Master," Lucia greeted, jumping to her feet. "The new slave is finally awake. She calls herself Pelonia. She's weak and the medicine I gave her has run its course."

"Then give her more if she needs it."

The man's deep voice poured over Pelonia like the soothing water of a bath. She turned her head, ignoring the jab of pain that pierced her skull.

"You mustn't move your head," Lucia snapped, "or you might injure yourself further."

Pelonia stiffened. She wasn't accustomed to taking orders from slaves.

Lucia glanced toward the door. "She's argumentative. I have a hunch she'll be difficult. She denies she's your slave."

Silence followed Lucia's remark. Would this man who claimed to own her kill or beat her? Was he a cruel barbarian?

She sensed him move closer. Her tension rose as if she were prey in the sights of a hungry lion. At last the lion crossed to where she could see him.

Sunlight streaming through the window enveloped the giant, giving his dark hair a golden glow. A crisp, light-colored tunic draped across his shoulders and chest contrasted sharply with the rich copper of his skin. Gold bands around his upper arms emphasized the thickness of his muscles, the physical power he held in check.

Her breath hitched in her throat. She could only stare. Without a doubt, the man could crush her if he chose.

"So, you are called Pelonia," he said. "And my healer believes you wish to fight me."

Her gaze locked with the unusual blue of his forceful glare. For the first time she understood how the Hebrew, David, must have suffered when he faced Goliath. Swallowing the lump of fear in her throat, she nodded. "If I must."

"If you must?" Caros eyed Pelonia with a mix of irritation and respect. With her tunic filthy and torn, her dark hair in disarray and her bruises healing, his new slave looked like a wounded goddess. But she was just an ordinary woman. Why did she think she could defy him?

"Then let the games begin," he said, his voice thick with mockery.

"You think…this…this is a game?" she asked faintly.

The roughness of her voice reminded him of her body's weakened condition—a frailty her spirit clearly didn't share. Crouching beside her, he ran his forefinger over the yellowed bruise on her cheek. She closed her eyes and sighed as though his touch somehow soothed her.

Her guileless response unnerved him. The need to protect her enveloped him, a sensation he hadn't known since the deaths of his mother and sisters. As a slave, he'd been beaten on many occasions in an effort to conquer his will. That no one ever succeeded was a matter of pride for him. Much to his surprise, he had no wish to see this girl broken, either.

"Of course it's a game. And I will be the victor."

Defiance flamed in the depths of her large, doe-brown eyes. She didn't speak and he admired her restraint when he could see she wanted to flay him.

"You might as well give in now, my prize. I own you whether you will it or not."

He gripped her chin and forced her to look at him.

"Admit it," he said. "Then you can return to your sleep."

She shook her head. "No. No one owns me...no one but my God."

"And who might your god be? Jupiter? Apollo? Or maybe you worship the god of the sea. Do you think Neptune will rescue you?"

"The Christ."

Caros wondered if she were a fool or had a wish for death. "Say that to the wrong person, Pelonia, and you'll find yourself facing the lions."

"I already am."

He laughed. "So you think of me as a ferocious beast?"

Her silence amused him all the more. "Good. It suits me well to know you realize I'm untamed and capable of tearing you limb from limb."

"Then do your worst. Death is better...than being owned."

Caros suddenly noticed Pelonia had grown pale and weaker still.

He berated himself for depleting her meager strength when he should have been encouraging her to heal. He lifted her into his arms.

She weighed no more than a laurel leaf. Had he pushed her to the brink of death?

Holding her tight against his chest, he whispered near her ear. "Tell me, *mea carissima*. What can I do to aid you? What can I do to ease your plight?"

"Find...Tiberia," she whispered, the dregs of her strength draining away. "And free me."

* * * * *

Will Pelonia ever convince Caros of who she is and where she truly belongs? Or will their growing love bind her to him for all time?

Find out in
THE GLADIATOR
by Carla Capshaw.
Available in November 2009
from Love Inspired® Historical.

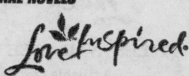

TITLES AVAILABLE NEXT MONTH

Available October 27, 2009

TOGETHER FOR THE HOLIDAYS by Margaret Daley
Fostered by Love
Single mother Lisa Morgan only wants to raise her son with love and good values. Yet when a world-weary cop becomes the boy's reluctant father figure, Lisa discovers she has a Christmas wish as well....

A FAMILY FOR THANKSGIVING by Patricia Davids
After the Storm
Nicki Appleton may have to say goodbye to the sweet toddler she took in after the tornado. Yet when the man she once loved comes home to High Plains, can she count on Clay Logan to be her family for Thanksgiving—and forever?

CLOSE TO HOME by Carolyne Aarsen
Jace Scholte was the town bad boy—until he fell for Dodie Westerveld. But instead of marrying him, Dodie ran away without a word. Now, they're both back in town. But Dodie still won't talk about the past....

BLESSINGS OF THE SEASON by Annie Jones and Brenda Minton
Two heartwarming holiday stories.
In "The Holiday Husband," Addie McCoy's holidays have never been traditional. Could Nate Browder be the perfect old-fashioned husband? In "The Christmas Letter," single mom Isabella Grant's dreams of family come true when a handsome soldier comes knocking on her door!

HIS COWGIRL BRIDE by Debra Clopton
Former bronc rider Brent Stockwell doesn't think *ladies* belong in the pen or his life. But cowgirl Tacy Jones has come to Mule Hollow to train wild horses and she's determined to change his mind—and his heart.

A FOREVER CHRISTMAS by Missy Tippens
Busy single dad Gregory Jones doesn't have much time to spend with his sons. When Sarah Radcliffe tries to teach him that love and attention are the greatest Christmas gifts of all, will he realize his love is the perfect gift for Sarah as well?

LICNMBPA1009